Tightrope

Ash Marah

Credits:

Early reading: Leane Green, Natanya Sheaves, Gabi Brockelsby, and D.W illiams.

Cover Design: DMWilliamsphoto Photographer & Cover Design

Editor: Jennifer Griffin

Blurbs

When Being Trapped Can Lead to Pleasure.
  Eamon
I was the head of a big corporation and a family legacy secret society that had infiltrated key positions around the world to manipulate events for their own agendas. My life was dangerous, and enemies could be anywhere, waiting to bring me down.

But all of it was a lie, the strong person I portrayed wasn't me at all, it was a front.

I craved something different. It was dangerous, but I couldn't get it out of my mind.

Until I found details of a resort in the Caribbean called Leather Persuasion, their motto was 'Where BDSM is a way of life and fantasies unfold.'

It was an opportunity to live out my fantasy. It was a risk, but for once I was going to put my needs first, even if it killed me.

Jarrod
My day job was an assassin for a well-known mercenary group. I knew who Eamon really was, and I planned to get answers from him about my family.

I would use anything at my disposal, even following him to the Leather Persuasion Resort, and look for opportunities to have him at my mercy.

We explored our kinks, and the sexual chemistry between us exploded whenever we were together. I can't let down my guard and let him in. He's the head of the enemy, and he was hiding information I needed.

Can I ignore the intense feelings that have developed while we have been exploring our sexuality? Our enemies were closer to us than we knew, and a wrong step could see us both dead. When things turned ugly, we need to work together to survive.

Can the enemy become a savior?

Or the downfall of us both.

To my best friend Leane,

We never needed rope to keep us together. Friendship like ours is unique and special.

You have always shone brightly with beauty, heart and talent.

For every life milestone you were there either holding my hand or being my cheerleader.

I am glad I have been able to broaden your knowledge in all things romance and the fun we have had exploring.

This one's for you babe, our friendship rope is strong and will never be broken.

Love Ash

Also by Ash Marah & The Leather Persuasion Series

AZ Demons Series

Killer Vibes- AZ Demons Book 1

Russian Roulette Vibes- AZ Demons Book 2

Mischief Vibes- AZ Demons Book 3

Mystery Vibes- AZ Demons Book 4

Xmas Vibes- AZ Demons Book 5

Leather Persuasion Series 2026

Consenting by D.Williams

Contents

Prologue

Eamon

Today was my fifteenth birthday. There were no presents, cake, or fanfare, just an empty tomb of a house with impersonal servants who I didn't know after spending most of my time away at boarding school. Our Greenwich house was modeled after an estate in the English countryside, with manicured gardens and even a stable. Not that I had ever seen a horse near the place. It was impersonal and cold, like my parents had treated me for my entire existence.

My parents' wing of the house was off-limits to me, and I was happy to stay well clear. My mother rarely got out of bed. She spent most of her time in her suite of rooms, and the only people who ever saw her were two of the servants. I had made the mistake of forcing my way into her room once, only to find she couldn't even string a sentence together. She preferred to live in her own world of alcohol and prescription drugs. I could hardly remember what she looked like now, having not seen her for years. I knew she was alive, though, because I hadn't been dragged to a funeral, and my father would make sure that happened to keep up appearances.

I was home for the summer, and boredom had set in. Today there would be a break in the schedule of doing nothing because my father had summoned me to his Manhattan office. I was under no illusion this visit was about him celebrating my birthday with me. I gave up that hope around age seven, when year after year I'd thought things would change and my parents would celebrate my birthday like other kids at my school, but every year, there were no cake or presents unless they were needed for a photo opportunity—and then they'd probably been purchased by my father's staff. I never went without the latest technology, but even that would have been about appearances.

My father never really socialized with his peers outside business meetings and lunches. I'd never been welcome in the social groups of rich kids my age, and if anyone tried to befriend me, it was because they wanted something. It had taught me that you couldn't rely on anyone. To protect myself, I'd isolated myself from the kids who lived in the mansions around us and the ones who went to my school.

My father wasn't abusive. He was just never around or active in any part of my life. I always felt like a robot that was stored away in the cupboard until someone remembered to take me out to charge.

Being home for the summer break meant I was trapped in this large house with nothing to do. I didn't even have my studies to occupy my time. I was slowly going crazy.

After dressing and then eating breakfast, a man I had never seen before drove me into Manhattan. Father's summons had set my teeth on edge—this was only the second time I had been to his business headquarters. Why now?

Finally, we entered an underground parking garage. The drive had been made in silence, and I'd had too much time to overthink the situation. I took the elevator to the lobby. The building was in an expensive part of town, and the furnishings and decor matched, with plenty of marble and a massive glass art piece suspended from the ceiling. Everything was shiny and expensive. I was met by a concierge staff member and redirected to a different elevator that I knew went only to the top floor. Only the best penthouse for my father. All this was done in silence. Had everyone in Father's employ taken a vow of silence or something?

When the doors opened, I was greeted by a woman I knew was Father's executive assistant. She was framed in the doors like she was on a catwalk. "Hello, Eamon. It's nice to see you," she said. A blonde who had perky tits I bet were man-made, she was as plastic as the rest of the people Father surrounded himself with. I wish she had kept quiet.

I nodded. Why break my silence now? I noticed she'd had her lips done. Probably to suck my father's cock harder. I knew she did more than shuffle papers around.

"Follow me." She turned to her right and sashayed away from the front reception desk, where another blonde with big lips was sitting. That must be a company perk; either that or the plastic surgeon had a two-for-one sale. I walked behind bimbo number one down a corridor that had lots of doors with name plates on them.

The royal blue carpet was so lush it was like walking on a manicured lawn.

I bet the art on the walls was from some rich ass who splashed paint on a canvas and was paid millions for his originality!

The lady walked to the end of the corridor and opened a door. "You can wait here."

I had been directed to a reception area outside my father's office, which I remembered from my last visit a few years ago. I had only been here that time because Mother had been "sick." More like she'd overdosed and been taken to the Betty Ford Clinic.

The assistant kept walking and knocked on one of the doors, entering without waiting for a response.

"Eamon is here," I heard her say.

"Bring him straight in."

I walked into the office. It was a big room, with a solid wooden desk and a small boardroom table and chairs that seated twelve people, and it had a view of the Manhattan skyline. Everything screamed old wealth.

Father didn't seem happy to see me, so why the fuck did he summon me like I was his minion? I took a seat at the table, and he came and sat opposite me.

"Eamon, I need you to pay attention."

No how are you or happy birthday. What, did he think I was still five? What the hell? I nodded.

"Our family can trace its lineage back several centuries in Europe, prior to our immigration to America. We had to build our empire here, ensure our power and destiny. Many in our line had a head for business, and we formed partnerships with other first families."

He was staring at me intently. "A secret group of powerful men formed an alliance they called the Velatus Deus."

I nodded. I had no idea what he meant, but I would Google the term later. No need to drag this out, earning more disapproving looks and sitting around listening about a bullshit secret society with weird handshakes. I could read a Dan Brown book for that.

"The Velatus Deus looked after our own interests by infiltrating and manipulating every layer of society, placing our pawns in places where important decisions are made. Along the way we created enemies, people who wanted to stop us. We couldn't show our hand, which is why we operated in secret. Do you understand what I'm saying?"

Father had stopped for dramatic effect. What was there to get? Secret society, powerful, and everyone hated you.

I noticed he'd changed the narrative to we, so I didn't think a nod was going to cut it this time. "Yes."

"What I'm going to show you must be kept secret, and you are not allowed to tell anyone. Not your mother nor your friends. It is important you understand, this can only be discussed with me."

He looked different now, a zealot vibe around him, his eyes burning intently into mine. This story was starting to make me nervous—I had a feeling this was not just a tale but more a legacy. I swallowed the saliva building in my mouth.

"Yes, sir."

He got up and walked to a wall in his office, where he moved a side table. There was an electrical outlet behind where the table was, and he put his thumb in between the holes on the outlet and held it for about five seconds. The wall started to move, creating a small walkway.

It was a secret hideaway. Shit just got interesting. I jumped up, wanting to explore what was in there. I followed Father into the dark room, and lights came on as we crossed the threshold. The room was long and narrow, filled with shelving that held archive boxes, what looked like artifacts and antiques , and books. I wanted to explore to see what they were and what purpose they had being locked away. A desk down at the end held TVs with security screens and a computer. There was a lot of stuff crammed in here, and it would take a considerable amount of time to go through it all.

Once we walked in, Father pressed a button and the door closed behind us. The lights were enough to see in front of you but still created shadows, giving the room a sinister feel.

Father turned to face me. "I'm the head of Velatus Deus, and this is your legacy."

A secret society with a room to explore? At the time, it had seemed like a great adventure for a boy who led a very boring life. Father spent the next two years teaching me what it meant to lead Velatus Deus and respect the legacy. I'd felt the walls closing in on me. I hadn't wanted this life. I'd had other plans. By the time I was seventeen, my father was dead, taken out by an assassin. The adventure at fifteen had turned into a nightmare. All my hopes of getting out of the leadership position were sunk as my father bled out on the pavement. My mother overdosed a day after my eighteenth birthday. It was like she'd hung on to get me there, then I was on my own.

Father's legacy was money dripping with blood and layers of Machiavellian-level bullshit that took years to unravel. My loneliness became a way to survive, and the sexual urges that had built as I'd gotten older had to be repressed. I had a corporate image to protect, and as the head of my family business and the Velatus Deus, I had to always watch my back, or I would be the legacy's next victim.

Chapter 1

Eamon

I was punching the bag set up in my home gym at my Greenwich house hard enough to make it swing madly, causing the chain connecting it to the ceiling to clink and groan. I needed to burn off some of this aggression. I had already gone through four personal assistants this year and it was only April. It wasn't that I was abusive, but I was a workaholic, and I expected my personal assistant to be available when I required them. I knew I was a grumpy bastard and hated dealing with the social niceties that people expected. It all seemed a waste of time.

My last personal assistant had screamed at me that calling at two in the morning was not acceptable. I'd thought she had staying power, but she'd only lasted a week longer than the others.

When I got engrossed in my work, I didn't watch the clock. Running two organizations—one a secret to the world—was time consuming. Sleep wasn't something I always had the luxury for.

Throw in my grumpy asshole personality and apparently there wasn't enough money in the world to make my personal assistants want to work for me. That was another thing one of them had said as he'd walked out the door.

Sweat dripped down and stung my eyes. I had to exhaust myself until I fell into bed, tired enough to sleep. This was what my life had come to.

Over the years, sex had helped as a distraction, but picking up prostitutes randomly wasn't doing it for me anymore. I'd had to rely on them so my enemies couldn't set me up, but even that formed a pattern if you looked hard enough.

The real reason sex no longer worked for me was my secret urges that were a contradiction to the way I looked and the person I portrayed to the outside world. All of my life was a lie. I couldn't show any vulnerabilities, as that could get me dead, so I kept living half a life, never being fulfilled.

I'd finally exhausted myself enough to shower and drop into bed. Sleep didn't come easy, and when it did, my dreams were about rope and hot men in leather.

The next morning, I got up early and made my way to the office. I drove myself, my bodyguard beside me. That was something I couldn't negotiate away, but damned if I was going to be driven around by a silent driver like I had growing up. The commute from the Greenwich house was long, but I preferred it to the Manhattan apartment. The house might be big and empty, but it was all I knew and where I'd spent my childhood. The apartment still felt like Father's even after I had it redecorated. His office was the same—I had made some changes to the carpet and furniture, but I still felt like an imposter and that the space wasn't my own.

I got in before everyone else—only the security team seeing me—and worked at my desk. Once it was a respectable time, I called Human Resources. When the phone connected, I got to the point. "Ms. Griffin, do you have a replacement personal assistant for me yet?" My tone was tart. I had to call them, which pissed me off.

There was a slight pause. "We're working on it."

She was probably concerned it would have to be her if she didn't find someone.

"Well, get someone up here to empty the outbox and have the work done. I shouldn't have to state the obvious."

I knew I sounded pissed, but the workload wasn't going to stop and they should have thought of that.

"I suggest you work this out immediately."

"Yes, sir."

I ended the call and let my cell thump onto the desk.

This company had been in my family for generations, and we dealt in imports and exports of different types of goods around the world. Most of the business was legal, other than a small illegal element linked to the Velatus Deus. I dealt with that part directly, and the work was done by a different team than the one handling the company's legal ventures.

I looked over to where I knew the secret door was that my father had shown me when I was fifteen. The Velatus Deus sacred documents and journals were in there. I had always wondered why they weren't in a buried bunker somewhere. According to my father, we needed to hide in plain sight, and the information needed to be accessible without tipping anyone off. Since the entrance was in my office, no one could see me enter or leave the vault. It was fire protected and acted as a safe room as well as storage. All of that didn't save my father, though. He was gunned down on the sidewalk in front of the building in broad daylight when I was seventeen.

A knock on the door pulled me out of my heavy thoughts.

"Come in."

A girl I didn't recognize came in and emptied my outbox. She didn't say a word or make eye contact. Had I become that much of a tyrant that people treated me like a wild animal who would attack without provocation?

"Thank you."

She looked up, startled, and shuffled out the door as fast as she could. Fuck, maybe I was the world's biggest asshole.

This office was filled with expensive furniture and art, but it was still a prison. One I was starting to resent.

A sigh left my lips. I really needed a vacation. I opened my locked drawer and pulled out the glossy pamphlet that had been sent to the alias I had created.

A tropical paradise in the Virgin Islands looked back at me. Trunk Bay was home to a secluded resort called Leather Persuasion. I had been looking at this pamphlet for months and putting it back into my drawer, not having the courage to take what I wanted for myself. Not throwing the information away was telling in its own way.

The Leather Persuasion Resort specialized as a discreet place for the BDSM community to explore their sexuality with like-minded people.

The question I kept asking myself: Could I break away from the chains of my positions as CEO of my company and head of the Velatus Deus to be someone else and finally get to experience the part of me I had never been able to let out?

My head was busy as all the thoughts about why this was a bad idea swirled around my brain. There was a risk of exposure, but more importantly, the greater concern would be my personal safety. My alias, Eamon Campbell, was not a millionaire, therefore he wouldn't require a security detail or be armed to the teeth. This Eamon was a guy from the burbs who liked bondage and power dynamic games. Nothing more than that.

Could I do it? Was I prepared for the consequences if this went wrong? I was at the point where I was willing to take the risk.

I slapped the pamphlet into my left hand. "Fuck it, you only live once, right?" Now I was talking to myself.

This had a higher chance of blowing up in my face than the average Joe, but I definitely needed a vacation. Otherwise, I didn't know what would happen if I lost control. I logged on to the resort's webpage and registered. I filled in a questionnaire, which was problematic in itself. Should I be honest about my needs and what I was looking for? If I was only going to do this once, I wanted it to fulfill all my fantasies and have no regrets.

I threw the pamphlet back into my drawer and locked it. It was done. I needed to pack before I talked myself out of it. *Trunk Island, I'm on my way.*

Chapter 2

Jarrod

I'd been tracking Eamon Blackwood for four weeks. Other than going to the office and back to his gated estate, he didn't do much else. I knew his driver doubled as a bodyguard and there were at least two guards on at night, but that was it. The other staff at the estate were not live-in—they came and went. It looked like the housekeeper did all the shopping and prepared his meals.

I was perched in a tree at the rear of his property with my binoculars, hoping to see something that would give me some insight into the man. For someone with his money and resources, he was boring as fuck.

The biggest shock to my system was Eamon being a good-looking bastard. He was tall and built, with sandy brown hair and green eyes. The ass on him was tight and looked like a perfect peach. Watching him exiting his pool while water dripped down his torso made my cock hard enough to hammer nails. I had to remind myself why I was here, and it wasn't to ogle and drool over Eamon Blackwood.

He was the enemy, and all I needed from him was to lead me to the Velatus Deus so I could bring it down piece by rotten piece. Just as it had destroyed my heart.

The security around his office building and the number of guards they kept on after business hours made it tough for me to break in there. A hacker friend was helping me attempt to break the security system around his home, as that looked like the best option to snoop around and try and get some information on the guy. His security system was good, but I was told it could be hacked—it would just take time.

I was usually a get in, get out person. The tech work would've already been done, and I would come in and use my sniper rifle to take out the mark. This job was personal. I had a mission, and I wanted revenge. Taking Eamon Blackwood out from a distance wouldn't do the job. The Velatus Deus would just replace the head of the snake and carry on like they had for hundreds of years. They had ideas of grandeur, naming themselves the veiled gods in Latin. If I was Eamon's security, I would not be giving a sniper like me all these opportunities to take him out. Was he that arrogant or just been provided with poor security advice?

I knew all about how the Velatus Deus operated. My father was part of the organization, and he had just as much blood on his hands as the rest of them.

My phone buzzed in my pocket. I put my earpiece in and answered the call.

"I've found a back door into the security system through maintenance coding, but this guy is good. I can only get you a small window of time before it will reset itself and come back online," Ben, my hacker, said.

Ben and I went way back, having gone to school together as kids. We had kept in touch and helped each other out when we could. I knew that he messed around doing some black hat work, but I didn't ask any questions.

"What sort of time are we talking?"

"I would say thirty minutes tops."

"Ok, I can work with that. You work on making sure all angles are covered, and I'll put together the entry plan. Thanks, and good work," I said.

Ben sighed. "I just hope that my help isn't going to see you dead. The Velatus Deus don't muck around. Their enemies don't normally see the light of day. I've always imagined a row of people in cement shoes on the floor of the ocean."

That was disturbing. He should lay off watching *The Sopranos*. "Ummm... not sure what to say to that other than they would never leave evidence around. Also, thank you for your help."

Ben clicked his tongue. "I can see that I can't convince you to leave this alone."

That would never happen. To my dying breath I would have my revenge. The Velatus Deus took something from me that broke my heart and they would suffer.

"No, and you know why."

Ben exhaled loudly. "Yeah. Okay, I will do everything I can to make this as airtight as possible."

I needed him to come through for me. "Thanks, Ben. I appreciate you being a good friend."

"Well, I hope you're not going to be a dead friend. Bye."

The line went dead. *I hope that too, Ben!*

Eamon went inside, and I only got glimpses of him when he was framed in a window that faced the wooded area I was hiding in.

Not long after, I saw him drive out of his garage and down to the public road. I knew he would be heading to the office. I would wait until Ben called.

My phone vibrated, and I answered. "Get in place and I'll tell you when," Ben said.

"Okay."

I climbed down from the tree and walked to the area of the wall I had marked to climb over. I had a small grappling hook and rope that I would use. I dusted myself off—I didn't want to drop leaves around in this mausoleum of a place. It would be a dead giveaway that someone had been here. I bet a speck of dust wouldn't dare settle on the furniture.

I left the line open so Ben could still talk to me in my earpiece. I waited for his instruction. I hoped it was a short wait, as I was feeling exposed standing crouched beside the wall.

"Go."

I threw the hook and it attached on top of the wall, and I quickly shimmied up and over. I left the rope on the inside so I could repeat the process on the way out.

I got to the rear door of the house and used my lockpicks to open it, and then I was in. They'd relied on the electrical system and not the locks.

It was like walking into a showroom. You could tell the furnishings were expensive, but everything was sterile and cold, with plenty of marble and glass fixtures. A few plants were the only thing that livened the place up. The inside lacked personality, and there were no family photos or mementos. Even the carpet was white. I popped on bootees over my shoes so I didn't track dirt from the woods throughout the place.

I made my way through the estate as fast as possible, mindful of the time limit. I walked up the stairs in the middle of the house, finding bedrooms. The main bedroom was more of the same, with no personality. Even the suits were hung together by color. The color scheme of the room was forest green and black. Luckily the walls were white or it would have looked like a dungeon.

The next door I opened was an office. This room was different—it was styled with a man in mind. It had forest green carpet, a dark brown sofa, and a heavy wood desk that dominated the room. You would need six guys to move that fucker. No personal items could be seen. There weren't even any art or decorative items to lighten the room. It was actually depressing.

The top of the desk was empty. Eamon must have taken his laptop with him, as I hadn't seen it anywhere on my walk around the house.

"Fifteen minutes left," Ben said in my earpiece.

I sat in the desk chair and tried to open the drawers, but everything was locked.

I used my lockpicks again and I was able to disengage the locking mechanism.

I didn't see anything worth hiding in the drawers. A few pens, a highlighter, and a stapler. My eye went to a glossy pamphlet showcasing a tropical island. I pulled it out to find it was for a resort called Leather Persuasion in the Virgin Islands. Reading on, I discovered the resort specialized in BDSM, the guests were matched according to preferences, and it was a safe place to explore your sexuality.

Why would Eamon Blackwood have this in his drawer?

I pulled out some papers that were the only other things in the drawer and realized they were travel arrangement documentation to the Virgin Islands and a confirmation for a reservation to the Leather Persuasion Resort for an Eamon Campbell. I had no idea why Eamon would take the risk of being on an island with limited ways on and off, but this was my way to get close to him to get some answers.

I took photos of all the paperwork. It looked like I would be sunning myself on a tropical island. I'd get Ben to help me make the appropriate reservations and ensure our questionnaires matched. On paper, Eamon and I needed to look like we were compatible and had the same interests.

It was the perfect opportunity to get to Eamon, and I was excited for the chance to get the first loop around the neck of the Velatus Deus.

Chapter 3

Eamon

I was able to get a direct flight to Miami, and then it was a seaplane journey from Virginia Key to St. John Island, where Trunk Bay and the resort were located. The plane was a small ten-seater—not my preferred way to fly. I hated being squeezed in like cattle. As the plane approached land, the turquoise water was so clear I could see the abundance of colorful fish swimming in their simple and uncomplicated life, the fields of coral throwing off prisms of color. The island's mountains and hills were covered in lush vegetation, and there was a good aerial view of the resort nestled on the beach when the plane banked to land.

The resort was spread out along the beachfront. The main hotel complex, consisting of regular hotel rooms, was in the middle, with cottages spread out left and right from the center. The cottages ranged from smaller and simpler in layout and furnishings to others that were more luxurious. The activity and playrooms were directly behind the main hotel complex. There were even designated outdoor play and exhibition areas marked on the map, and guests were allowed to go naked anywhere on the resort grounds.

The plane pulled up alongside a pier. There were other towns on this island, but Leather Persuasion Resort, which was on the north side, kept everyone's arrivals and departures discreet. I stepped off the plane with the other vacationers, the sunshine warming my back, and I looked over at the beauty of the pure white sand. I knew there were many hiking trails through the dense tropical vegetation, and I was looking forward to jogging outside rather than on the treadmill I was used to in my home gym.

We were greeted by a blond guy wearing a Leather Persuasion monogramed button-up shirt. I made my way to the guy and noticed the other nine people did the same. There were at least two couples, but the remaining five didn't seem to know each other. One was a hot guy as tall as me with black hair and blue eyes. He definitely worked out—I could see muscles under his shirt—but overall he wasn't as big as me. He looked good in his tan colored shorts and cream polo shirt.

I got caught checking him out and he gave me a flirty smile. I didn't want to just pick up a pretty face though. I was determined that all my fantasies would be played out during this visit. If I only got this one chance, then I was going to live it my way, and that meant not playing the role that most people assumed of me.

The guy from Leather Persuasion stood in front of us, and he had a huge grin on his face. "Hello, and welcome to Trunk Bay. I'm Lance, Director of Guest Relations, and I will be your host with the most. I'll be escorting you to the Leather Persuasion Resort and making sure your stay is comfortable and everything you imagine. A little rope burn or marks are an optional extra."

There were a few laughs from the group.

"Please leave your luggage, and we'll load that for you. Follow me to your new home for the duration of your stay."

We followed Lance to a tricked-out Mercedes van. He had a good suntan, and his hair never moved, even when the coastal breeze picked up. With my long legs, I made it to the van first and eased my way in to sit on the longest seat with the widest leg room. Mr. Hottie flopped down beside me. I stared out the window, only getting a glance of him in the glass's reflection. I could feel the heat of his leg pressing up against mine. I didn't know what his aftershave was, but it was manly and musky. I had to stop myself from taking deep breaths to draw his scent in. The van set off and I was able to concentrate on the scenery to distract myself.

Lance sat up front, opposite the driver. It wasn't long into our drive when he twisted around to face us. "Okay, lovely people. I will be handing back questionnaires for you to fill out. You gave us some basic information when you booked, but now we need the nitty-gritty. We need to know how to fulfill your wants and needs and keep you safe. Now remember, folks, your experience at Leather Persuasion is only as good as your honesty."

Why did I feel like he was looking at me when he said that? He wasn't—it was just my paranoia. Lance handed back clipboards with pens attached. The questionnaire was only two pages, and for most people who were up-front about their sexual wants, it would have been easy for them to fill out. This was the moment of truth, where I made the choice of being honest about my needs. It was harder to write than I thought because the man I portrayed and my sexual needs didn't match. In this case, being vulnerable could get me killed.

I was conscious of the man beside me. I doubted he would be what I was looking for, which was a shame. He really was a fine specimen of a man and he smelled amazing.

Fuck it, go big or go home. I had never been a coward, so why start now? I was going to do it! I angled the clipboard toward the window and answered every question honestly. By the time I'd completed it, we had arrived at the resort. I was glad. My skin was crawling and I needed to be out in the fresh air. Not touching the Hottie would also help with the static electricity that had started firing around my nerve endings. We all piled out of the van and handed our clipboards to Lance, and he took a quick look at each one as they were handed over.

He raised his eyebrows at mine and gave me a blinding smile that would have made a toothpaste commercial executive excited. "Mister Campbell, you will be having a great time, and this is the perfect place to make your wishes come true."

I nodded. I felt like saying it wasn't Disneyland, but I kept my grumpy opinions to myself and walked to the reception desk to check in. I had managed up until this point not to engage in any conversation with the staff or guests. I was disassociating from the beautiful tropical location and needed to snap out of it.

At the reception desk, there was a bright, bubbly blond woman there to greet me. "Mister Campbell, we hope your stay at Leather Persuasion lives up to your expectations. Here is a map of the resort and a list of activities for the next two days." She placed the map on the counter. "We are here, and I've marked your cottage. Your luggage will be taken there. Here are your keys, and Lance will be in touch to coordinate your personal activities. We hope you have a great stay."

"Thank you."

I looked down at the map and walked south of the main hotel complex. Cottages were scattered along the beachfront, some facing the beach directly and others set back but still with ocean views. My cottage was toward the end of the row farthest away from the main hotel complex and set back, but I still had direct sight of the ocean. I had deliberately picked the middle of the range accommodations, cost-wise, more in keeping with what Eamon Campbell could afford.

It was still nicely appointed and had a king-size bed. Everything was well maintained and looked like it was put together by someone who knew what they were doing. The air conditioning had already been turned on, which was a relief from the humid tropical heat.

I looked at the list I'd been provided with. There were two pages—one was the typical games and water activities you would get on any Caribbean resort vacation, and the other one had things like bondage exhibitions and *How to Whip Your Partner with Finesse*.

Even though it had been a long day of travel, I still had this itching sensation under my skin. Going to bed and having an early night did not appeal. I checked the program, and a demonstration of Shibari bondage was about to commence in twenty minutes, giving me just enough time for a quick shower and a change of clothes.

Once showered and dressed, I checked the map and headed toward the community space building, which was directly behind the main hotel complex. This was the first time I would see something like this live. Anticipation made my pulse race. I'd finally made decisions about things I wanted to experience rather than what was required from someone in my position.

When I walked in there were about twenty people already seated in front of a small black dais. The room itself was plain, with white painted walls, and there were rows of hard plastic seats set up facing the dais. I noticed the hottie from earlier was here as well. I looked away quickly so we didn't make eye contact. I made sure to sit away from him, as I didn't want him to see my expressions or note the hard-on I was sure to get from experiencing something that lived in my fantasies on many nights in my cold bed.

I sat down and tried to relax my muscles. A man and lady came out and stood on the dais. The man wore loose black pants and a tank top and the woman was naked. She was of average height for a woman and had a toned body, with firm, high breasts and a shaved pubic area. From her confidence standing in front of others naked, you could tell she had done this many times before. The man was middle aged, with gray filtering through his dark hair. He was a little larger than the lady. I didn't think he was as fit or exercised as regularly.

"Welcome, everyone. My name is Master Lee, and Veronica has agreed to help me today. I wish to emphasize that you should not try Shibari unless you are fully trained or being supervised by a Master," he said.

Veronica lay down on a table that was covered by a white sheet, and Master Lee started to tie thin ropes around her torso.

"The ropes we use are called Asanawa. Shibari is not just bondage, it is art. We are looking to display the body in aesthetically pleasing formations."

I watched as he started forming the patterns, and all I could think about was how I wished it was me who was being tied up. I wanted to be submissive and at the mercy of my master. My cock was hardening not from watching them, but from imagining it was me up on that platform. Just looking at the ropes made me want to squirm.

"Today we will be demonstrating the reverse Shrimp Tie. This means instead of the legs being tied at the front, Veronica will be face down and her legs will be bent upward."

Once Veronica was on her stomach, Master Lee started to tightly form all the connections so that she had rope around her upper chest and under her boobs. The lower ropes tied around and secured her hands crossing over and held tight against her back. There was rope around her stomach that went down splitting the lips of her vag and back to the same rope that was above her ass.

I was having trouble controlling my breathing. My cock was so hard, I worried I was going to shoot in my shorts without even touching it. I had to stop thinking about those ropes caressing my skin like a lover and the pulling of those ropes straining my muscles until I arched into an unnatural formation.

A rope was tied around Veronica's ankles and then tied to a rope under her ass cheeks. The art piece was complete and she looked beautiful, her body twisted and manipulated into that formation.

"Always check that none of the skin is showing signs of lack of circulation. Don't rely on your partner safe wording. Many people go into subspace early on when being tied like this and might not be in a position where they can be responsible for their own well-being.

"Okay, for the finale. We take the rope from the ankles along the back and it looks like a tie at the end. We are going to have the rope go around Veronica's mouth and link it with the rope that is along her back. Any pull of the ankles will also pull against Veronica's mouth and neck."

Fuck, I had to pinch my dick to keep from orgasming. Would I be able to have this or would my head get in the way of what my cock wanted? I really wanted to do this. I wanted to feel the ropes and the burn of strained muscles. I would be my own piece of art crafted with my body.

I glanced sideways and met the eyes of Hottie. We stared at each other, not able to look away. He had a look of hunger on his face. Was that for me or the ropes? I licked my lips, and his eyes followed the movement of my tongue. The pulse in my neck fluttered and my cock throbbed. I didn't think I had ever felt this aroused. Hottie was nearly as big as me and would be able to dominate me physically. Would he be the one who could make my fantasies a reality like I wanted?

Chapter 4

Jarrod

The resort was well organized, making check-in effortless. The location was beautiful, with white sand and clear blue water, and cocktails were free and plentiful. What more could you want? Except for me... I wanted answers, and I wasn't going to let the scenery, including the gorgeous Mr. Blackwood, distract me from my purpose.

I discreetly followed Eamon to his accommodations so I would know where his cottage was located. Mine was in the same row, with three cottages between us, just as Ben had arranged. I really owed him big after this. If I came out the other end alive, I'd need to square all the favors he'd done for me.

I didn't know what activities Eamon would be interested in. For now, I'd attend everything on the program until I knew his habits better or I could get information from his questionnaire.

There was a daily BDSM activities program, and the first major activity that started soon was a Shibari demonstration. I got ready and walked to where it was being held.

My phone vibrated in my pocket, so I pulled it out as I was walking to find Ben calling.

"Hey, what's happening?" I asked.

"Well, I have some good shit to tell you. I was able to hack into the resort's system, and they just updated the questionnaires you all filled in. Your mate Eamon wants to be a submissive and experience rope and whip and flogging play," Ben said.

Fuck, that wasn't what I was expecting. It didn't gel with who he was and the lifestyle he showed the world. I'd thought he wanted to come here for the opposite—to dominate someone and bleed off some of his pent-up frustrations.

"You there?" Ben asked.

"Yeah, sorry. I was just taking it in."

Ben laughed. "This might be easier than you think. Accidents happen."

"Thanks."

I ended the call. This information was a curve ball, and I needed to recalibrate. Getting to the Shibari workshop now had a higher importance. I hurried along the path through the tropical garden to the room the demonstration was being held in. People were just taking their seats, but I didn't see Eamon. It was possible he might have crashed after the long day.

Just when I thought he wasn't going to show, he walked in. There were a few seats near me, but he chose to sit on the other side of the room, slightly in front of me, and I could see the side profile of his face.

Master Lee and his volunteer Veronica were introduced. I had dabbled in the BDSM scene a little back home. I had a membership to a club, but I wasn't a regular. I didn't want to be tied down with a submissive, and if you went all the time and they knew your face, they could be persistent. Being submissive didn't mean they wouldn't go after what they wanted, and not everyone lived the life twenty-four seven.

The rest of the room was silent, respecting the Master and the type of rope play. Lust filled the room like a tangible thing that could be cut with a knife.

I had performed Shibari over ten times, under the supervision of the Master at my club. Once this demonstration started, I spent most of the time glancing over at Eamon. His facial expressions went from arousal to full-blown lust. He was fidgeting in his seat, and watching him was making my cock hard. I had to remind myself I wasn't here for that—he was the enemy—but my dick had a mind of its own, and watching Eamon Blackwood unravel was one of the sexiest things I'd seen.

The thing that really pulled on me was the desperate want that was all over his face. Like a kid who was only allowed to look in the window of a happy family on Christmas morning. This wasn't just something he wanted to try—it was something that, deep down in his psyche, he needed to feel complete.

People around me were openly pleasuring themselves or each other. Everyone was still respectful to the Master, keeping their noises down to soft moans and sighs.

The demonstration was winding down, and I couldn't take my eyes off Eamon. He was struggling to control his emotions and body reactions. I could see the muscles in his neck contract as he swallowed. He licked his lips in an attempt to stop them going dry.

He looked over and caught me staring at him. We maintained eye contact. There was an intimacy about it, like we were the only two in the room. I had seen his vulnerabilities, and I needed to use them against him. I knew he was into guys from my research, but if I hadn't, I would have worked it out from his stare.

When the demonstration was over, Eamon jumped up like his ass was on fire. I was closer to the door and able to fall into step behind him. He had no way to get away from me—everyone was in vacation mode and not in any hurry.

The humid tropical night air hit me as we left the air-conditioned room. I reached out and touched Eamon's arm, and he flinched, spinning around quickly to face me.

I put my hands up. "Sorry, didn't mean to startle you."

He frowned at me.

"Hi, I didn't get a chance to introduce myself before. I'm Jarrod."

I put my hand out to shake.

He looked down at my hand like it was poisoned.

He finally reached out and took my hand in his. His skin was smoother than mine but not as much as expected. He had calluses in the same places as me from repetitive weapons training.

"Eamon." His voice was gruff, and he had a neutral look on his face. People were squeezing past us, pushing us closer together.

This was actually awkward. Gone were the looks of longing and arousal he'd had during the show. His mask was back in place. Still, I needed to plant a seed. I kept repeating my mantra: *Don't forget my goal.*

I gave him a big welcoming smile. "I noticed you enjoyed the Shibari demonstration, and I just wanted to put out there that if you're looking for someone to work with, I would be open to it. I would be happy to be your dominant if you wanted a safe space to explore."

I could see his face close up and all expression leave it. "Why would you think that's what I'm looking for?"

It was time to make a tactful retreat. He may want it, but was he going to allow himself to have it?

"Either way is fine. I just thought we shared an attraction, but if I got that wrong, I'm sorry. I'll leave you to it."

I smiled and walked away. He didn't stop me, but I slowed down so he could see what room I was in. He might give in at any time and I wanted him to know where to find me. I could feel the heat of his stare, so I knew I was still in his line of sight. I didn't look back. When I got to my door, I swiped the lock with my card and walked into the air-conditioned room.

The sight of his face rattled around in my head for hours, keeping me from sleeping. I had to remind myself why I was here, again. It wasn't like me to think about someone so intently, and even more so when on a mission that was important to me on a personal level.

I tossed and turned all night, sleeping in broken periods. I got up early so I could watch Eamon's movements, as I planned on setting up a camera and bug in his room once he left for breakfast. I might hear something useful if he made any calls about Velatus Deus business. Any intelligence could help me plan my way forward.

I watched him walk past, and I quickly left my room. I had no time to waste before either he would be back or the cleaning staff would start their morning room schedule. The coast was clear, and I confidently made my way to his room and swiped a master key I had stolen yesterday. His room was identical to mine. I planted the camera in a bushy tall plant and the bug under the desk. Next, I went through his bag. He had unpacked his clothing and hung it up neatly. There was another zipped-up bag as long as my forearm sitting on the floor of the closet.

I unzipped it to find a treasure trove. There was a compact whip made of soft leather strips, a ball gag, pieces of rope long enough to tie up arms and legs, and a bottle of aloe vera lotion. He had thought of everything. It was all quality gear, new, and didn't have any scuffs or usage marks. I didn't think Eamon had done this before, and just thinking about him at my mercy was making me hard.

I started visualizing using the items on Eamon—having him at my control and doing what I told him. I started to sweat, and all my blood went to my cock. I was so hard, my dick was tenting my shorts. Fuck my life, why now! I needed my dick to get on board with the agenda, which was not to dominate Eamon Blackwood while I got off and forget he was a dangerous man. Betrayal had already happened, and that was why I was here.

Jarrod, you idiot, you need to torture this bastard for answers and then kill him, not fuck him!

Chapter 5

Eamon

I was able to get some rest, but I'd tossed and turned most of the night. Breakfast was in a big dining room that you shared with the other guests. Nothing fancy, just wooden tables and chairs and a buffet that was good and plentiful. I was sitting at a table by myself, nursing a coffee, listening to the sounds of cutlery clinking and people having conversations around me. None of the other guests came anywhere near me—I must have been putting out *fuck off* vibes.

My mind was occupied with thoughts of Jarrod and his offer. We definitely had sexual chemistry, that wasn't an issue, and he was the type of person who I pictured in my fantasies. When it came down to reality, though, could I let him dominate me? I needed to remind myself that was why I was here. Was I going to go home with my tail between my legs and not experience my sexual fantasies at least once? Why the hell did I risk it all and come here if that was the case?

Veronica walked into the dining room, and people said hello to her like they were all best friends. I guess when you saw someone naked and tied up, you knew them better than just waving to your next-door neighbor. There was no judgement or embarrassment. Instead, everyone was congratulating her on a great show. I kept forgetting this was supposed to be a safe place for people to explore their love of BDSM.

Lance made his way around the tables, grin big and a preppy attitude, and he sat down in the spare chair at my table. "Hello! How is everything? Do you have everything you need?"

I needed to stop being an idiot and get on with my purpose for being here. "If I wanted to do a private scene but still wanted supervision, how would I organize that?" I asked before I could chicken out.

He smiled wide. "You have come to the right person. Did you have someone in mind for your second?"

"Yes, Jarrod." Just saying his name made my heart rate speed up.

Lance bit his lip and raised his eyebrows up and down repeatedly. "Ah, nice choice. We can have a Master either in the room or viewing remotely to ensure that everything is safe and done correctly. What scene takes your fancy?"

All my blood headed south to my cock. While I loved ropes, there had always been one thing that had been my number one sexual fantasy. "Flogging on the Saint Andrew's cross."

Lance's eyes widened and he fanned his face with his hand. "Oh, that sounds yummy. You're in luck. Master Michael will be doing a demonstration this afternoon, and you can see him in action and decide if that is for you. He's one of our best."

I nodded. It was all I could do because words had escaped me. My cock throbbed, and I needed a hot minute to calm the fuck down.

"Fabulous. I'll be back in touch after the demonstration and you can let me know what your pleasure is."

"Thank you," I squeezed out, my mouth dry.

"Okay, have a great day, and we'll see you at two p.m." Lance jumped up with a bounce and then he was off to talk to other guests.

I left the dining room and walked out into the humid air, heading back to my room so I could try to relax. I opened my laptop to check emails and I couldn't concentrate. An hour later, I changed into shorts, a tank top, and tennis shoes, then started a run on one of the many hiking trails before heading along the beach, enjoying the view of the ocean. There weren't too many people around yet, as they were probably sleeping off a night of cocktails. The sun still had a bite this early, and with the humidity, I was lathered in sweat. In a few hours, the beach would be full of guests lying on daybeds, the air filled with the scent of coconut sunscreen, and bodies red not from bondage but from overindulgence in the sun.

I went back to my room, showered, and tried again to keep myself busy with work emails. I wasn't very successful—it took me twice the time it would normally. Any time I thought about the flogging class, my cock started to tingle and thicken. I was glad when it was time to get ready and head out.

I changed into compression underwear under my shorts and a T-shirt that was a little longer to try and contain my dick. It was the best I could do to control my erection. I had to do something because my cock wasn't listening to me!

I walked over to the exhibition room listed for this activity. Would Jarrod be attending today? If so, I'd be able to gauge his interest in this type of BDSM. I knew deep down in my psyche that pain was my kink, and being restrained at the same time was the ultimate fantasy. I loved the idea of rope play, but the pain of that restriction wasn't enough to flip me into subspace. I realized I needed a more physical and acute pain along with rope play to hope to achieve that state of mind. That had only happened once to me, which was when I found out about my pain kink. I had decided to cut myself to get a sexual high off the pain. I hadn't known what I was doing enough to do it safely and went into subspace with open bleeding wounds. The drop was dangerous, since I'd had no one to care for me—to tend to my wounds and mental health. I now knew why aftercare was so important.

I entered the room and about ten people were seated already. "Hello, sit anywhere you like," a lady wearing a Leather Persuasion polo said.

I looked at the people already sitting, and none of them were the handsome Jarrod. I had the pick of seats, so I sat against the wall, that way I'd only have someone on my right.

Everyone was smiling and greeting each other as new arrivals came into the room. I gave a nod to anyone who caught me looking at them. I tried to loosen my muscles, as I could feel myself tensing up. I had to remember I was on vacation and should be relaxed from all the kinky sex I was having. Everyone else was carefree, enjoying the sun and cocktails. If I didn't fit in, people would look too closely at me, and I didn't need that.

I looked forward, not wanting to catch anyone's eye so they didn't sit beside me. The Saint Andrew's cross stood prominent on the dais. The cross was the more traditional type, made of white wood, and was a little more hardcore in that it had no padding like you now saw in the modern constructions. There was leather buckle cuffs attached to chains at each of the points of the cross for your wrists and ankles. The chains were lowered and tightened to adjust for people's variance in heights. In the BDSM community, the cross symbolized surrender, vulnerability, and trust.

The saliva dried up in my mouth and my skin itched. This was my fantasy come to life. The only way this could be more perfect would be if I was the person who was going to be tied to the cross. My dick started to chub up. Fuck! This was before the show even started.

I felt the air next to me change and I smelled Jarrod's musky, manly cologne before I looked sideways to see him. Just that on its own sent my pheromones jumping for joy. I turned to the right and Jarrod filled the seat beside me. When our eyes connected, he smirked, and I couldn't help but smile back. This man was hot with a capital H. Dressed in khaki shorts and a light blue polo shirt, the humidity had put a slight curl in his black hair, and I wanted to run my fingers through it. I laced my hands together in my lap so I didn't reach out. Today was about teasing my senses and enjoying the visual eroticism of BDSM.

The rest of the seats filled up quickly around us. Two men and a woman walked out on to the dais. The woman was naked, and the men helped strap her wrists into the restraints and then her ankles. She was average height and build for a woman, with brown hair she had put up in a messy ponytail on top of her head. One of the men stepped down and walked to the back of the room and the other faced the audience.

"Hello, I'm Master Michael, and I've been involved in BDSM for over twenty years."

Possibly in his forties, Michael had looked after himself and had a fit, lean body, and there was a little gray sprinkled through his short brown hair. He was an attractive man but not in Jarrod's league.

"My lovely assistant today is Penny. We will demonstrate how the cross is used and also the technique you need when using a flogger. This is not something you should just start doing. You need to first do your research and be taught and supervised by a master. This can be dangerous and can cause serious harm if not done correctly."

Did Jarrod have any experience? He carried himself like this was not all new to him. The thought of him with a flogger in his hand made my dick fill with blood. The compression underwear was strangling my erection. I hoped they stopped my pre-cum from making a wet spot on my shorts.

"Are you okay?" I turned to Jarrod, and he was looking at me with raised eyebrows. I hadn't realized that my fidgeting was noticeable.

"Fine, thanks." *Eamon, fucking get a hold of yourself.* It was like once I'd stepped onto this island, I'd become someone else. All my cool, calm, and collectedness had left me and I was like that fifteen-year-old again who was wide-eyed about the secret lair with treasure. I had a plan, but this was ridiculous. I was the CEO of a large trading company and the leader of a secret society. I was not a twelve-year-old who jerked off all the time and couldn't help getting hard-ons.

"Penny and I have already spoken about her desires, boundaries, and safe word. Don't skip this important part of play because it is essential for healthy and safe bondage."

Master Michael talked about feet positioning and areas of the body that should be avoided. Once he picked up the flogger—with its leather strips and sturdy handle—and got into place behind and a little to the left so the room could see what was happening.

I imagined myself up there and Jarrod standing behind me without a shirt, slapping the flogger into his hand, and a whimper escaped me. I refocused on the couple in front, taking shallow breaths to try and calm down. The hairs on my arms stood on end, I was so wired.

Master Michael connected his flogger to Penny's back, causing a slapping sound. I jumped in my seat even though I was expecting it. There were sounds of excitement from the crowd as each hit landed.

He kept up a steady beat, moving up and down her back and ass. Penny was arching her back and moaning. You could see vertical red and white lines covering her torso, her skin striped perfectly.

The couple in front of us was excited, the lady jumping into the man's lap in the reverse cowboy position. She had her legs spread wide, and he fingered her pussy while they were both enjoying the show. A few minutes later, she stood up, he lowered his shorts, and she climbed onto his dick, rocking on top of him like she was on an amusement ride.

I licked my lips. I wanted that to be me on the cross. Jarrod widened his legs and his thigh bumped mine. I gave him a quick sideways glance. Fuck, his cock was hard, and from what I could see, Jarrod was not lacking in the size department. I bit my lip, then realized I had been staring for too long. I raised my eyes until I reached his. He was looking at me, his eyes laser focused on mine. The background noise of people fucking and moaning faded away and lust surrounded us in a bubble.

I pinched the skin of my palm to try and calm down, but it wasn't very successful considering I liked pain. Finally, I pulled my eyes away and looked forward. I had trouble focusing on what was happening on the dais, my was cock hard enough to hammer nails and throbbing. I wanted to touch it but couldn't in front of Jarrod, I wasn't that far gone that I wanted to be on the person on exhibit.

Master Michael rubbed the handle of the flogger back and forth between Penny's legs. She threw her head back and orgasmed with a loud squeal.

Master Michael presented the flogger handle. "Look how wet Penny was." You could see moisture clinging to the handle. She didn't do it for me in any way—I was turned on by the flogger and the marks it left on her body.

He went back to his table and picked up a bottle of lotion, returning to Penny to spread it over her back. She was then taken down, and Master Michael talked about aftercare. He sat in a chair and pulled her into his lap with his arms around her.

I wanted this, and Jarrod was the only person I had seen who came close to my fantasy. I turned to find him already looking at me. "Would you be my Dom? I want a turn on the cross."

He studied me for a few seconds, trying to read my face. I knew I didn't look like a submissive. If he hadn't offered, I wouldn't have thought I was a match with him.

"Yes."

That one word was powerful and blew my mind. I had to get out of here. The walls were closing in and I needed some fresh air. Now that I had made that next step, my stomach was cramping and I felt nauseous.

"I'll talk to Lance to organize it," I told him, then I got up and rushed out the door.

I walked along the beach to gather my thoughts and calm the fuck down. The man I was in my everyday life had been left on the mainland. This Eamon was someone else I didn't recognize. I'd finally gotten the balls to take something for myself, but at what cost to my sanity?

Chapter 6

Jarrod

I just watched Eamon leave the room like his ass was on fire. The picture I had of him and the reality were miles apart. Where was the stone-cold killer who was the head of the Velatus Deus?

I got up and walked outside. I really needed to get my head in the game. I decided to work out, hoping it would help, so I went to my room and changed into my gym gear. They had a decent facility at the resort. After all, horny people had to burn off their buffet meals and cocktails so they could get laid.

Once I was there, I started on the treadmill to give myself an opportunity to get my priorities straight. Eamon was hot and got my dick hard, but he was still a killer. Nothing had changed about the reason I was here. I needed to build his trust in me, then he'd let down his guard and I'd have a good opportunity to find out the information I wanted.

Monsters came in all different sizes and looks. Eamon's looks and his actions while here might portray a certain person, but that wasn't what was inside him. His blood was black. Velatus Deus dealt in death and they were ruthless. For a second there, I'd forgotten that he was the head of the snake and I had declared him my enemy.

After finishing my workout, I was back in the right headspace. My mission needed to continue, and I planned for it to be successful. It was personal, and I wanted my revenge.

I went to the main dining room for dinner. Eamon wasn't there. A few people asked if I'd like to be part of their planned events, but I politely declined and told them I had plans, though if anything changed, I would get back to them. You never knew when you might need an alibi. Otherwise, all my attention would be on Eamon. He was the reason for me being here.

When I got back to my room, there was a fancy mono-grammed resort envelope that had been pushed under the door. I opened it and took out the single page that was inside.

Dear Jarrod,
You are cordially invited to a scene with Eamon.
When: Tomorrow
Time: 2 p.m.
Room: Saint Andrew Room
Scene: Saint Andrew's cross with you as the Dominant.
Your scene will be supervised by Master Michael.
If you wish to decline,

please call me.

**Lance,
Leather Persuasion Resort**

My cock throbbed. I looked down at it. *You need to behave. This is a job, so stop enjoying yourself.* I think I might be spending too much time on my own because I was now talking to my dick. I shook my head and got into the shower.

Once I was redressed, I checked my messages and video called Ben.

"Yo, how's life playing dominatrix master."

I laughed. "You idiot, a dominatrix is a woman."

Ben started giggling. "Well, fuck, I had no idea. And what makes it worse, you don't like vaginas. That would be your worst nightmare."

I rolled my eyes. We liked what we liked. The smell and feel of a man was always what did it for me. A flash of Eamon popped into my head. I couldn't deny he was a fine specimen of a man.

"Any news?" I asked. Ben was still looking for information on the dark web for me.

"Not on Eamon, but something is happening with your father. He's been having meetings around town. That in itself isn't what stood out. It was that he met with Boris Ugov, who has ties to the Russian Bratva in New York. The Velatus Deus and them have butted heads for many years and they have a cold truce."

That was strange. I knew my father hated the Russians. I used to hear him curse their name regularly when I was growing up.

"Maybe it was business for VD?" That was my nickname for them, since they were like a venereal disease.

Boris was more of a henchman for the Bratva. If it was Velatus Deus business, my father would have met with the inner circle, and I think Eamon would have been involved, considering how tenuous their truce was.

"The street cam footage I got of them, they were leaving a café. Then they started having an argument and pushing each other around. Both their guards didn't step in, like it was a normal occurrence and they had instructions not to interfere."

That was weird and not like my father, but he and I weren't close. He was a manipulative bastard who had made mine and my brother's childhoods a nightmare. From my research, I knew my family had been part of Velatus Deus since its conception, when we'd stepped onto US soil. What made it interesting was that it wasn't from my father's side, it was my mother's. Somehow my father had weaseled himself in, and it all seemed to happen after my mother's oldest brother was killed. I'd always found that a very convenient opportunity for daddy dearest, as he just stepped up and filled the void. If my father was at my back, I would expect a knife, not support—that was the type of man he was.

"Keep an eye on it and see if there is any chatter on the dark web."

It sounded like Eamon might have a traitor in his midst, and Father might be making a power play. That would be more likely than any of the other scenarios that were going through my head. I could be biased because I expected the worst from my father and it could just be normal Velatus Deus business.

"Will do, Daddy Dom."

I gave him the middle finger and ended the video call.

As the eldest, I'd caught on very early that my father couldn't be trusted. I'd played the game until I was eighteen, and then I'd gotten out from under his thumb. Before I'd left, I'd collected contacts and people of interest who I could turn to. Sometimes they didn't work out because Father got wind of it, but I had lucked out with a group of mercenaries who had taken me under their wing and I'd never looked back. When your best skill was shooting the wings off a fly, you could command top dollar in the open market.

I went to bed and got up early for a jog along the beach and then had breakfast. I had to run to burn off the good food they served here, needing to stay combat fit. When all this was done, I still had a job that I wanted to get back to. After breakfast, I kept myself busy trying to distract myself from this afternoon. Thinking of Eamon tied up and at my mercy got my heart rate up and my cock throbbing. It surprised me I wasn't dizzy from lack of blood flow to the rest of my body. Why couldn't this asshole be a balding old guy with a paunch?

Finally, it was time to get ready and head out. I dressed in my loosest shorts because I was going to need the extra space for my dick; otherwise, I was going to cause myself an injury. You could actually break a cock, and I didn't want to experience that!

I looked up on the resort map where the room was and headed out. Locating it, I opened the door to find Master Michael and Eamon were already there and a cross had been set up. Or maybe it stayed here permanently for private play? It looked the same as the one from yesterday—white wood construction with chains and leather cuffs and no padding.

Eamon gave me a small smile. He looked nervous. I could tell this was not his normal scene, and considering his job, that wasn't surprising. I would bet my sniper rifle that this was his first time on the cross. The thought made me excited in a primitive way, like when you got to plow virgin ass. Come to think of it, had he let anyone fuck him before?

Jarrod, get your mind in the game or this will be over before it starts.

"Ah, here is your partner today," Master Michael said. He put his hand out and I shook it. Master Michael had a good skin care routine, as his skin was soft and supple. Weird, the stupid shit that went through your mind when you were trying to direct your thoughts away from your cock exploding.

I had to clear my throat with a small cough. "Nice to meet you."

Eamon stared at me, his face neutral. It was the face I expected he used in the boardroom. I hoped that wasn't his O face. I wanted to know he was enjoying my attentions.

"Okay, I've read your questionnaires, and Eamon has filled me in about his preferences. Jarrod, I see you have some experience," Michael said.

"I had a previous partner who was interested in this type of scene and we had started to explore. I still have an active membership at a BDSM club back home."

Eamon's eyes burned a hole in the side of my face. I hoped I got to see that intensity during our scene. Dominating a strong man like him would be orgasmic.

"I will leave you both to talk through your limits and safe words, and I'll keep to the background. I will only intercede if I think something is unsafe or your actions are heading toward breaching your set limits."

We both nodded our agreement. We had already signed the waivers and they had all our preferences. I just needed to confirm the details with Eamon.

I walked over until we were only separated by about three feet. "Have you done this before?"

"No," he said. He sounded like he was saying no to a glass of water.

That primal side was coming out in me again. I loved that I was going to be his first. Also, I had a feeling he would be able to tolerate a lot of pain. Yesterday, I could see in his eyes how sexually worked up he was. He wanted this fantasy badly.

"Tell me your limits." He couldn't hide the look of excitement reflected in his eyes.

"Nothing below my upper thighs, stay within the normal back and ass area, and no blood."

That was very basic as limits went. I needed to know more about how he wanted me to act in this scene.

"What do you want from me? Is dirty talk okay? Do you want a Dom/sub dynamic?"

These scenes were not just about the flogger and the restraint. Our minds heightened our arousal and helped us slip into subspace.

Eamon looked shocked, like this had never occurred to him. "Anything is fine. I don't have any preferences."

That wasn't how this usually worked, but I was here to get close to him, not to become his lover.

I nodded. "Safe word?"

"Virtus."

That was Latin. I think it translated to mental strength, courage, and worth. As kids, we were forced to have Latin language lessons because the Velatus Deus used Latin to converse like the elitist group of assholes they were.

Eamon walked over to the cross and started unbuttoning his shirt. His skin was tanned and his chest was lightly sprinkled with brown hair. The man must regularly work out because he had defined pecs and a decent six pack. With his height and looks, Eamon was any man or woman's wet dream. He was a sexy fucker. If you could get past the outer ice to the fire within, he was one of the most attractive guys I had ever seen.

He unzipped his shorts and let them drop to the floor, leaving him in red Speedos. They cupped his juicy ass and highlighted his large cock. My mouth filled with saliva; I could imagine his cock sliding in and out of my mouth, choking me. While I had Dom tendencies, I loved to suck cock, and I could deep throat with the best of them.

"Jarrod, are you ready?"

I came to. I had just been standing there in my daydream while Eamon waited for me to attach the leather buckle restraints that connected to chains. I wanted to squeeze my cock to relieve some pressure, but I didn't want to highlight how hard I was just from him dropping his shorts. A Dom should have more control than this.

I walked over and attached the restraints. "Comfortable? Not cutting off blood flow?"

"They're good, thanks." He looked good, and I totally wished I had met him under different circumstances.

The man was facing the cross, spread-eagle like an offering to the gods, restrained by his wrists and ankles. It was heady, having him in my power. He was tense, all his gorgeous muscles flexing, and his ass was a perfect peach that I wanted to bite. I stood admiring his perfection. We had a witness, so today would not be the day I got my answers.

I approached the table holding three different-sized floggers. I picked up the middle one; Eamon was a big man with wide shoulders.

I walked up behind him. "You need to relax or this isn't going to work," I whispered in his ear.

He shuddered, and then I saw him trying to relax his muscles one at a time.

I assumed the position and the correct stance—behind him and to the side—ready. He was, too, or as much as he was able when he wasn't used to submission.

"You will call me Sir, and you can only speak when I say you can. Nod if you understand."

He nodded. I hadn't gagged him, as I wanted to hear what came out of his mouth during this scene and also have the opportunity to punish him if he misbehaved. I raised the flogger, ready to start.

Eamon tensed up. "Relax your body," I whispered again. Real damage could happen at the muscular level if he didn't.

There was still some tension, but I was able to commence. The flogger handle was hard in my hand, and the leather strips were braided and the length of my forearm.

I let loose, and the slap of the flogger hitting his skin was loud, echoing off the walls. He arched like he had been struck by electricity and moaned like a person in rapture.

I started slowly, with minimal force, until I could see what his tolerance was like and what he enjoyed as far as force went. His skin glowed a soft pink from his shoulders down to his lower back, and his cock tented his Speedos, which were barely containing him.

"Do you need it harder, like the naughty boy you are? You may answer," I said softly.

We hadn't talked about him having humiliation kink, but it just felt right.

"Yes," he said in a quiet voice.

"Boy, when I want an answer, I expect it to be loud and for you to address me correctly. If you don't want this to stop, you need to answer me. I hear it in your voice that you want this, you grub."

Eamon took a deep breath. "Yes, Sir. Thank you. I want this, and I would like it to be harder please."

"I'm only doing this because I want to punish you and not as a reward."

I flicked my wrist and used more power so the braids whipped down, leaving welts along Eamon's back, making the pink turn red. There were no breaches of the skin or bruising I could see. No matter my reason to be here, I took this part of our BDSM experience seriously,

He arched as much as he could, throwing his head back and making a mess of his lip with his teeth.

"You love this like the fucked-up boy you are. You're dirty and nothing. You only live to serve me."

He moaned as I continued down to his lower back. He was beautiful in his submission. I didn't think I had seen anything more beautiful.

"Boy, do you wish everyone could see you looking pathetic, moaning like a whore, your back all red?"

"Yes," he moaned.

I pulled down his Speedos in the back and slapped him hard on the ass with the flogger. I nearly moaned with him, my cock so hard it was becoming painful, and I couldn't give it a few tugs to help ease it. I was the Dom and needed to show control and constraint.

"I didn't say you could talk, maggot," I yelled at him.

The Speedos couldn't hold the hardness of his cock, and it peeked out of the top. It was so erect, his foreskin was pulled all the way back, his cock purple and painful looking. My dick had its own heartbeat, it was throbbing so hard. At this rate, I might come before him. The sight of him restrained and aroused was like catnip to me. His back was pretty, my marks glowing under the bright white lights. I had done this, and I loved to see my work all over him.

"Have you had enough, you weak and pathetic piece of shit?"

Chapter 7

Eamon

Weak and pathetic echoed around in my brain. Every word out of Jarrod's mouth in that sexy gruff voice he'd deepened to make those comments went straight to my cock.

If anyone spoke to me like that outside this room, they wouldn't be breathing for long. Why did I love it while I was feeling the pain from the flogger working up and down my back?

The sting was exquisite, every nerve ending sending electrical pulses throughout my body. My cock was so hard it was becoming painful. All I could do was lean into the pain and enjoy the way it was making me feel.

Jarrod walked around in front of me. He stared into my eyes, then he used the handle of the flogger to run under the length of my dick. He wasn't gentle, and the harsh leather on my sensitive skin nearly tipped me over the edge and made me shoot. I had to show him I could be a good boy and only come when he let me.

He sneered at me like I was shit on the bottom of his shoe. "That looks painful. Do you expect me to touch it? If you can't come hands free, then you won't come at all."

A shiver erupted over my body. I wanted his hands on me, but if I demanded anything, this scene could stop. I hadn't come hands free since I'd had wet dreams as a teenager, and even then, I'd probably touched my dick in my sleep.

Jarrod cupped the back of my head and pulled me toward him. His mouth met mine hard. This wasn't romance, it was teeth and aggressive tongues. The sexual tension between us erupted, our tongues dueling for supremacy.

He pulled back, both of us breathing heavily. We stared at each other, aware of the chemistry that was between us. I think we were both shocked at the intensity of our lust. I saw the change come over Jarrod's face as he slipped back into character.

Now his face was stern. "Who am I?"

I needed him. My balls were painful and I wanted to come. I panted with lust and my need to submit.

"Sir."

"I'm in charge. Say it," he said in a raised voice.

"Sir, you are in charge," I said, my voice husky and cracking at the end.

"You, boy, have been bad and haven't kept to your place, like the filthy scum you are."

He went back to his position behind me and whipped up and down my back and ass with the flogger harder than he had before. I knew I could safe word, but I wanted it to burn. I wanted to feel it for days every time I moved.

My mind emptied of any thoughts, and all I could feel was the flogger working me over. The pain built, like a classical piece of music performed by an orchestra before the crescendo.

I was winding up tighter with each hit. I had never felt this level of arousal, every nerve ending was sensitive, fireworks were erupting all over my body. The pleasure was overwhelming my brain synapses. I couldn't hold back my orgasm.

My back arched as much as possible and I pulled tight on the chains holding me. "Fuck!" I yelled.

Cum erupted out of my cock in forceful jerks. The load was large, and with each pulse, my body felt like it was on fire. I slipped into nothingness, enjoying the feeling of total surrender. I floated in a sea of clouds, my mind at rest. I had never experienced this type of euphoria and relaxed state of mind before.

"Let's get you down from there."

I didn't know how long I'd stayed in the clouds before Jarrod spoke. His voice was the first thing to penetrate that place in my mind. I couldn't even describe how amazing it was, and even in my dreams I hadn't thought that this type of feeling was possible. He unbuckled the leather cuffs on my wrists, rubbing my hands to get the circulation going, and then leaned down to unbuckle my ankles.

"Come on, let's clean you up."

He led me by the hand over to a large couch and used one disposable cloth to clean up my cum and another to wipe my face. I had no idea that I had been drooling.

"Lean forward so I can get to your back. It's just aloe vera gel."

I did what he said, and he rubbed the gel all over me. It was cooling and took the heat out of my skin. He threw a small blanket over my nakedness.

He sat beside me and held my hand. I just lazed there like a sloth. It was like my brain cells had been scattered and I needed a hot minute to collect them for my brain to come back online. Maybe they shot out of my cock with my cum.

Jarrod handed me a bottle of water and I gulped it down. Now that I was coming back to myself, I could feel embarrassment settling in. Why did I respond to being spoken to like that? I didn't know what it all meant, all I did know was I had never come that hard before in my life, and it wasn't just about the pain. It was a combination of that, Jarrod, and the humiliation.

I watched Master Michael walk over to us from where he'd been sitting. I had forgotten he was even in the room, and that was why doing this at Leather Persuasion would be my only time. I couldn't afford to lose my sense of awareness.

"Boys, you have this under control. I have to say, that was hotter than the sun. Anytime you want to take that public, you give me a call," Master Michael said, grinning.

Did he still come in his pants like a teenager from just watching after all these years? He handed both of us cards with his number on it, and they listed his location as New York City. My heartbeat fluttered when I realized he was from my hometown, but I couldn't keep doing this. It left me too vulnerable, and in my business that would mean death.

I got up and dressed. Every pull on my back reminded me of what had just happened. The pain gave me orgasm aftershocks every time I made a move that made my skin ripple. I knew that I would bruise, and I was excited to see those marks on my body.

I looked over at Jarrod, and I had trouble raising my eyes. "Thank you, Sir. It was a good scene. I'm going to rest now."

I turned and was out the door at a fast pace. I needed the four walls of my room to ground me in the here and now. It was like I had multiple personalities that were totally different people. I got to my room and slammed through the door, then threw myself on the bed, back first.

Shit, that was painful. I was really fucked up. All the blood rushed to my cock, and it was hard enough to tent my shorts. I laid where I was, enjoying the uncomfortable feeling, and gave in to my hard cock. I unzipped my shorts until I could pull my dick out, and then I slid my hand up and down my length. I knew I wasn't going to get to the heights I had just enjoyed, but it would take the edge off.

I leaned over to my side table drawer, got out the lube, and squeezed some into my hand. I glided my hand up and down my cock, enjoying the tightness of my fingers. Every movement of my hand pulled on the skin on my back and it was delicious. I imagined Jarrod on top of me, holding me down.

"You've been a good boy, Eamon," he whispered in my ear. Then he bit down on my neck and collarbone, leaving marks for everyone to see that I was his. He owned every part of me. I was his boy.

My dick got harder as I imagined Jarrod in all his naked glory. I had only seen him with his shirt off, but that was enough to know he was fit and built. I wasn't that much bigger in height and body mass, and I loved that.

"Good boys get rewarded. Do you want my mouth around your cock?" I was going to hear that voice in my dreams for many years to come.

My cock jerked in my hand and Jarrod's mouth felt real. I couldn't hold back the moan that escaped me.

He slid down my body and sucked my dick into his mouth down to the root. He could take it all, and I could feel the back of his throat squeezing the head of my cock as I thrust in slightly, making him gag. His mouth was tight and rough, just how I liked it, and saliva dripped down my dick.

Pre-cum leaked all over my hand. I reached down and pulled on my balls, hard. The pain was exquisite, and my body shuddered from the pleasure. Then I came for the second time today. I panted as cum landed on my chest, nearly hitting my chin with the force. I lay there enjoying the afterglow of emptying my balls a second time.

"You're a good boy for coming when Sir said." Jarrod ran his fingers through my cum and lifted them to his mouth. He licked them like an ice cream cone, the point of his tongue gliding up each finger, making sure he got every drop.

"God, that man is hot."

The thought of this happening in the here and now sent me into hyperdrive. I couldn't afford to let my guard down because my enemies might find me here and use me for target practice. As much as I wanted to keep Jarrod, it couldn't happen. We had the next few days to explore and then I needed to go back to my life as Eamon Blackwood, CEO and leader of the Velatus Deus. The alternative was death. I didn't have any other options. This was the life I was born into, and there was no way out unless it was in a coffin.

Chapter 8

Jarrod

I had to keep reminding myself why I was here. It wasn't to make out with a hot guy, especially a hot guy who was my enemy. I needed to get my priorities right because I needed justice, and I was the only one who could get it.

When Eamon came, I did as well, in my shorts like a horny teenager. I needed to get back to my room and clean up. When I got there, I headed directly to the shower. While the hot water streamed over me, the memories of what just happened filtered through my mind like a slideshow. It had been one of the most sexually charged occasions of my life. BDSM and sex in general were going to have a hard time topping that moving forward. I had a bad feeling that this experience with Eamon was going to be the pinnacle, and it was going to be hard to find someone else with whom I'd share the same sexual chemistry as I did with him.

He was sex on a stick. Eamon needy and wanting while being flogged by me was going to stay in my spank bank for some time. Dominating such a big man, and one who was also powerful, really did it for me. It was something I wanted to explore in the future, but that wouldn't be with Eamon. By the time we finished here, he'd hate me.

Loyalty to certain members of my family needed to come first. I had never been so distracted on a job before. I couldn't let Eamon seduce me—he represented everything I hated.

I had a plan and I needed to execute it soon. There were only four more days left on the island, and I couldn't let this opportunity get away from me. I had sodium thiopental in my bag, and while it wasn't the truth serum like they made it out to be in the movies, it did lower inhibitions. If I teamed it with a Shibari scene, I might be able to get Eamon in a vulnerable position. Once I took my shot, though, all would be revealed and the game would be up.

I went for a walk and ate dinner. Before taking my chances to get the information I needed, I wanted to have a final memory of Eamon under my control. I dialed reception and asked to be put through to Eamon's room.

"Hello."

"Hi, Eamon, it's Jarrod. Would you be interested in doing a Shibari scene with me?"

There was a small pause while I waited for his answer. My stomach clenched. Had he not enjoyed working together like I had?

"Yes. When would we do it?" He sounded like he was ordering takeout, dismissive and cold. If I hadn't seen for myself how he let himself go while aroused, I wouldn't have believed it.

"I'll call Lance and see what can be organized. I have experience, and I'm confident that my technique is safe. Do you want a supervisor?"

I could hear him swallowing. I knew sex would be off the table if there was someone in the room.

"No, that's ok. You can text me when you know the details."

He listed off his phone number and disconnected. I found the card that Lance had given everyone on arrival.

Jarrod: Eamon and I would like to do a Shibari scene privately. Can you organize a room for tomorrow in the afternoon?

Lance: Of course, let me look at the room booking schedule. I will get back to you.

I did some push-ups to tire myself out. Nothing much was helping with distracting me from the huge erection tenting my shorts. When my phone buzzed with an incoming message, it startled me. *Jarrod, snap the fuck out of it. He is a guy you're using to get off and then you're going to use any method to get the truth out of him.*

Lance: We have a suitable room available for 2 p.m. called the Lotus. I have booked it for you. Happy hunting!

My stomach filled with butterflies—or they could be wasps, in this case. I needed to toughen the fuck up. I was only doing this to win Eamon's trust. If the little voice in my head whispered that I seemed to be organizing this scene for my own benefit, I told it to shut the hell up while I texted the details to Eamon.

Jarrod: Lance booked the Lotus Room for 2 p.m.

I just got a thumbs-up emoji in response, which was anticlimactic. I spent the rest of the night with my cock in hand while I imagined Eamon on all fours, my hand around his neck holding him in place as I fucked him hard. I knew he could take some punishment, so dream me didn't hold back. Sleep was hard to come by—*pun intended!*—even with tiring myself out.

The next morning I was up and at the gym early. I saw Eamon in the distance, jogging along the beach with no shirt on. That didn't help with the monster in my pants.

Luckily there weren't many people in the gym. I guess they threw their routines out the window when they were on vacation. I worked out until my arms and legs were spaghetti and then had a late breakfast. I was sitting at the table nursing a coffee when I saw Lance walking between the tables, greeting people. When he got to me, he sat in the spare chair beside me.

He gave me a cheeky grin. "You and Eamon seem to be hitting it off. I would like to be a fly on the wall later when you guys are together. I think there would be so much heat, my wings would melt off."

My face stayed neutral and I raised my eyebrows at him. I guessed tropical islands were still rife with gossip. He would see people come and go every week and probably imagined about their lives and what kinks they were into. I bet he had no idea what Eamon and I were keeping secret. In some ways, we were all trapped in different types of cages. Life wasn't one size fits all.

He smirked. "Oh, come on. You're going to top that hot tamale Eamon. I get the impression he doesn't let too many people do that."

If Lance only knew who Eamon really was and what he was capable of, he probably wouldn't be serving him up to me like a Thanksgiving turkey.

I got back into character and plastered a big smile on my face. "I'm treating this opportunity professionally. Eamon is a very attractive man, and I would love to do more than just rope play with him."

Lance's eyes widened and he looked up behind me. "Ah, Eamon. Come and take a seat."

Great... he just heard me. Or, this could be an opportunity to break the ice.

Eamon sat opposite me. I looked up at him and our eyes connected and stayed. He was hard to read, generally, except when heat and physical attraction bounced between us. That was loud and clear for everyone to see.

"Well, boys, I just got pregnant from that look," Lance said, sniggering.

I reluctantly pulled my eyes from Eamon and looked over at Lance. He stood up and leaned over like he had a secret to share.

"Boys, the Lotus Room is available at noon, if you would like to start this hotter than hell, scorching, cock exploding good time early!" Lance said before walking away with a sassy hip action.

And then there were two, the silence heavy and filled with sexual tension. I was aware of Eamon inside my space in a way I had never felt with another person. I had to remind myself this wasn't going to end well. In the future, once I'd gotten information from him, his eyes would turn to hate when they looked at me.

"Do you want to start at the earlier time?" I asked.

His stare would be considered intimidating, which was understandable in his day jobs. To me it was part of the appeal—tall, broody, and fuckable.

"Yeah, that would work." His voice gave me goose bumps.

That meant we only had an hour to wait. We sounded casual, but both of us were playing a part and hiding our true selves. I had an epiphany that we had been doing that our whole lives and it was something we had in common. If this was a real date, we would have been able to bond over our similar pathways in life.

I needed to set the parameters for this session. There were a few things to unpack—not only equipment but also boundaries. Shibari was usually done naked so that there was no chance of clothing getting caught in the ropes. I knew this would be our last session together. After this, I had to finish my mission, and any type of relationship wouldn't survive that.

"I want to talk about our limits for today." He nodded but didn't say anything. "I'll be doing simple formations of Shibari rope play. I want to know if things like kissing and touching of genitalia and or penetrative sex are acceptable."

I couldn't help but look directly into Eamon's eyes as I said this, and his facial expression didn't change. I could have been reciting a grocery list.

"I'm open to all those options as long as condoms are used."

Holy fuck. Getting in that tight hole was going to blow my mind. My cock went from semihard to rigid in a millisecond. I swallowed to get some saliva back into my mouth to be able to reply. I hope I didn't look like I wanted to throw him on the floor and have my way with him right here in the dining room. *Jarrod, stop thinking about your cock in his ass and get it together.*

I got air into my lungs without making it too obvious. "Agreed. We will also use the traffic light system as well as your safe word since we will be doing a variety of different rope and sexual play."

I hoped I sounded in control and confident. With all my blood heading south, my brain activity was on the fritz. This guy was working me both mentally and physically.

I stood up and turned slightly to the side to not give away how aroused I was. Eamon had one of his hands flat on the table, so I put my hand on his.

"Later."

I turned and walked away, trying to portray that I didn't have a care in the world. In actuality, my cock pulsed to its own beat and I needed to get my hand on it to relieve some pressure as soon as fucking possible. Once I was clear of the dining room, I fast walked like my ass was on fire to my room. I seemed to be doing this a lot lately, either to jerk off or clean myself off from coming.

Once I was in my room, I flopped backward and the hard wood of the door hit my back—it was all that was holding me up. I unzipped my shorts carefully and let them hit the ground. I had my hand around the head of my cock, spreading the pre-cum down my length, relieving some of the pressure. I closed my eyes and enjoyed the sensation of my hand gripping me tightly.

"Fuck yeah, Eamon. Get on your knees for me."

Eamon was quick to get on his knees, licking my balls while I stroked my dick. I felt his tongue lick the head of my cock and lap up my cum that I was squeezing out with my strokes. I stuck my cock in his mouth all the way to the back of his throat, cutting off his airway. His throat muscles spasmed on the tip of my cock. Eamon was making choking sounds, but I didn't care. He could take my cock until I came.

I let out a rush of breath as the pleasure hit all my senses. My imagination was strong, and the images played out like I could feel his breath teasing the hair around my dick. It didn't take too many strokes before my balls pulled up and my dick erupted, cum going down dream Eamon's throat. When I opened my eyes, Eamon wasn't there and I had sprayed cum all over the tiled floor that I now had to clean up.

I took a few deep breaths to calm my heart rate. Fuck, at this rate I was going to get calluses on my hands!

Chapter 9

Eamon

I stayed sitting at the table in the breakfast room after Jarrod had left. I was too in my head to get up and get breakfast. I couldn't believe I had agreed to sex while being tied up. Had I lost my ever-loving mind? There wouldn't be anyone there if he was too rough, and I would be at his mercy.

I shook it off and went to get food and coffee. While I ate, I thought about when I'd woken this morning. My back had been stiff and I'd had issues bending, but after my shower I'd loosened up some. I'd left my shirt off when I'd gone jogging, not wanting to get hard when my shirt rubbed on my sweaty back. The ongoing pain still gave me flash points of pleasure. Jarrod could get me to this state and I wanted to explore what we had.

Was I turned on by a hot man who made me think about bondage and pain every waking minute? Throw in the chance to bottom and my fantasy was complete. I couldn't turn this down from fear, only having one chance to experience this. Jarrod was everything I wanted in a man. Tall, built, and handsome, I needed his cock inside me, even if it was only once. I had promised this time to myself, and when I left the Leather Persuasion Resort, this memory would have to hold me for the rest of my life. I couldn't in good conscience bring someone into my life. Being openly gay might also bring its own challenges. As the head of the Velatus Deus, the traditional members were more likely to take me out than ask me to step down. I was letting the legacy die with me. There would be no children from my loins who would have to suffer like me. I refused to bring a child into this misery of a life. The other members could fight about it all once I was dead. I'd be at peace, and I also had a few surprises for the rest of the assholes who had made my life a misery. They said revenge was a dish best served cold. Nope, I may be burning in the fires of hell, but I was going to make sure I took them all with me.

I was going to take this opportunity and live my dream, for once putting my needs first. I got up and walked back to my room. I had some preparation to do if I was to lose my ass virginity.

I showered and cleaned inside and out. For the first time, my stomach felt restless. I wasn't one to let emotions rule me, unless it was annoyance and anger—I had plenty of that to share. I dressed in easy to get out of clothing and went commando. No point in underwear getting in the way when I had already agreed to penetrative sex.

I found the Lotus Room on the map and made my way there. I was starting to sweat, and I didn't know if that was from the humidity or my nerves. Giving total control over to a virtual stranger would be the hardest part for me. I knew to get what I needed that I'd have to shut down my fight or flight instinct to be able to really feel the power of submission. It was like two parts of my brain warring with each other.

I pushed open the sliding door to enter the Lotus Room, and the air conditioner breeze surrounded me in a cocoon of cool air. The room, which was as big as a very large bedroom, was empty except for a few tables and chairs pushed up against the walls and a couch. Jarrod was already here setting up the rope. I walked into the room, and he looked up and gave me a smile. He had a kit next to the rope that included safety shears, rope oil, and some steel carabiner clips. I could tell the rope was hemp, which was the best option for any rope play. He seemed confident, and the way he was arranging the rope, I knew he had done this before.

Sitting in the middle of the room was an armless wooden chair, and it looked like one you would see at any dining table in the suburbs back home—all wood, with a spoked back rest and legs braced by other wooden poles in a square under the seat. Jarrod walked over and stood in front of me. I could smell his citrusy bodywash or shampoo and the cologne he always wore. Both smelled sexy and would always remind me of him.

He stared intently into my eyes. "Are you ready for this? Do you want to change anything about our agreed upon limits?"

My brain had tried to talk me out of this, but it lost. "Yes, I'm ready, and nothing has changed since our earlier conversation."

Jarrod nodded, accepting me at my word. "What is your safe word?"

"Virtus."

He smiled at me, looking more relaxed than I had seen him before. "Good, and we'll use the traffic light system, if I feel I need an answer from you. The scene will stop if you don't answer or I'm concerned about any aspects of your safety. Do you understand this?"

"Yes, I do."

He knew what he was doing and was making me relax into the scene. "Okay, good. You're going to be draped over that chair face down. Your torso will be on the seat of the chair, and your arms and legs will hang down to the floor. You will need to remove all your clothing since we agreed to penetrative sex. Once I have all the ropes in place, it would be hard to get them out of the way."

My cock was starting to thicken just from the instruction discussion. At this rate I wouldn't be able to stop myself from coming before the first rope circled my body.

Fuck it! I was all in. I lifted my shirt up and over my head and unzipped my shorts until they were loose enough to drop to the floor. My cock was erect and jutted out from my body. I had to just own it or I would not enjoy this.

Jarrod approached me with a rope in his hand. "Eamon, you've been a bad boy. I don't want to but I'll need to punish you until I'm sure you know your place. You can only speak when I say you can." The gruff voice he used when chastising me sent shivers all along my skin.

He walked behind me, and I stood still while his hot breath hit the back of my neck. He reached around me to my cock and I felt his hand rub me. When I looked down, there was a white cock ring circling my dick.

"We would hate for you to come too early," he whispered in my ear. I shuddered, his raspy voice making all my nerve endings tingle.

He wound rope around my upper chest below my pecs, repeating this movement until my upper rib area was held firm with rope.

"What does that rope feel like, Eamon? Is it gliding over your skin like silk or prickly, teasing your skin just right?" he asked in a whispered sexy voice, then licked around the outside of my ear.

I shivered from his tone and the tight feeling of the rope. I had always wanted to feel this restriction.

Jarrod now circled my waist with a length of rope. Nothing was joined yet, but I knew that was about to change.

"I need you to lie down across the seat of the chair with your chest against the seat."

Once I was lying on the chair, the rope started to put pressure on my chest and waist. My knees were supporting my body, but I knew that would change soon.

Jarrod tied my wrists together and then fixed each elbow to the chair legs below my shoulders. He lifted my left knee and tied it to the leg of the chair at the wooden cross brace, repeating the rope tie on my right leg. Without my knees on the floor, I only had my toes to hold myself up. I was starting to feel the pressure of maintaining my balance and keeping myself in place. The ropes were firm, and every one of my movements pulled on ropes all over my body.

He stood in front of me and sneered. "How does it feel to be at my mercy? I could do anything to you and there would be nothing you could do but take it like the dirty slut you are."

My cock was pulsing to its own beat. Between the tight restriction of the rope, the comfort of being held securely—like a loving embrace—and Jarrod's sexy voice, I was finding it hard not to blow. Small beads of sweat dotted my forehead. Would the cock ring stop me?

Jarrod walked behind me and slapped my ass. "This all stops if you come, Eamon. You don't have permission to get off until I tell you."

He circled around me slowly, staring down at me in judgement. He slapped my arms and the backs of my thighs with his hand.

"Ah."

Jarrod shook his finger at me. "What did I say? No talking. If you want more, you need to behave."

I breathed deeply in an attempt to calm myself and take control of my body. I couldn't have him stop. I needed this. He hadn't even finished with the rope and I was in this state. Pre-cum was leaking out of my cock, tickling the sensitive head.

Jarrod picked up two lengths of rope. One he wrapped around his neck and the other was in his hand. He walked to me and used the length of rope in his hand to tie a loop from under my arm, down to my waist, and then to my ankle, pulling my foot upward. He repeated that on my other side with the length he had put around his neck. I was just able to get my big toes on the ground to help support my weight. This rope would stop me from straightening my knee in this position.

I was fixed into place. If I moved in any way, one of the other ropes tightened on me. My big toes were cramping from all the downward pressure I was exerting to keep the pressure off my knee ropes. I was well and truly fixed firm, what with the ropes to the chair and the ropes tied to different parts of my body.

Out of the corner of my eye, I could see Jarrod take off his shirt. He walked back and stood between my legs, staring at my ass.

"What color are you at, Eamon?"

"Green." I was living out my fantasy with a hot guy. I couldn't ask for more.

He grabbed my ass cheeks in his hands and squeezed hard.

I let out a moan. I couldn't help it. All the different sensations of restriction, pain, and arousal were sending me to a place I had never been sexually.

"Eamon, good boys get rewarded. You don't seem to be able to follow instructions, so you need to be punished."

I waited a few seconds, having no idea what was coming next. As my anticipation built, I had to remind myself to keep relaxed and not tense my muscles.

I heard the rustling of clothing, and I imagined Jarrod was unzipping his shorts and they were hitting the floor. He moved up beside me and I looked sideways. I was nearly in line with his cock. He was now naked, and his cock was plump and red. If I could lean toward him, I would have that juicy cock in my mouth.

"Eyes up here, Eamon." I looked up and Jarrod had a spanking paddle in his hand. I couldn't help it—my body shuddered in pleasure. The rope scratched my skin and squeezed me, reminding me I was at his mercy.

My eyes rolled back in my head, and I was panting heavily. "It wouldn't be much of a punishment if you enjoyed it."

I needed that paddle on my body. The rope was digging in just right and my muscles were straining, stuck in this pose I had been placed in that wasn't natural for me. The pleasure-pain feeling was keeping me in a state of arousal I had never felt before.

"Please, Jarrod."

He banged the paddle into the palm of his hand. The sound as it slapped against his skin made my mouth dry. He kept doing it until I wanted to squirm, but the ropes held me in position.

He leaned down right next to my ear. "I will not be gentle. I didn't say you could talk."

Fire rained down on my ass and my breath caught in my throat. I didn't have time to get in my head as Jarrod moved from my upper thighs to my ass, slapping me like he was playing table tennis. The bat was a totally different feel and sting compared to the flogger. The sting was exquisite and better than I could have ever imagined. I was shuddering in ecstasy.

"Ugh." I was trying not to make a sound, but I was slipping into subspace.

"Eamon, what is your color right now?"

It was like he was asking from a long way away.

"Eamon," Jarrod yelled.

That snapped me out of my stupor. I licked my lips to get saliva into my mouth. "Green."

He slapped me on the ass with the palm of his hand. My cock was hitting under the seat of the chair with every hit to my ass and was painful from the hard wood and from being erect for so long without relief.

Jarrod pulled on my hair, lifting my head, the position putting a strain on all the ropes wrapped around me.

"Do you want my cock up your ass pounding you like the whore you are?"

I started to pant again, and his words made extra pre-cum drip down the end of my cock. All I could think about was feeling his cock split me in half. I wanted this, and I was going to ride it out until there wasn't a drop of cum in my balls!

Chapter 10

Jarrod

"**F**uck me please."

I didn't think I'd ever wanted to hear three words so badly in my life. Watching Eamon let down his walls and submit was a thing of beauty. I knew what it cost him mentally to be this vulnerable. I had to remind myself that I would enjoy this moment, but then I had to bring back to the forefront of my mind who Eamon really was.

I moved to stand between his legs. He was spread out, served to me like a platter of the most expensive foods. It was risky to whip him again when he hadn't healed from yesterday, but I knew he would want it, and I kept it light. I ran both of my hands up his calves and thighs, and when I got to his ass cheeks, I pinched them hard enough to leave light bruises.

"Please," Eamon said, soft and broken, nothing like his assertive tone.

I started at the back of his neck and lightly kissed all the way down his spine, his skin forming goose bumps everywhere my lips touched. When I reached the start of his ass crack, I stuck my tongue in, swirling it around and teasing him with the promise that I would keep going and circle his hole.

Eamon breathing was erratic and he was shaking. More than likely, the stimulation of the flogging and rope work were sending him to new sexual heights of awareness. My cock throbbed and I wanted to get inside him before I blew all over the floor. I grabbed his ass cheeks and pulled them apart, diving straight to his hole and eating him out like he was an all-you-can-eat buffet.

"Ah, fuck, Jarrod."

His hole was pink and puckered. I licked around and then speared my tongue inside. Eamon yelled and jumped, but the ropes pulled him back into place.

He didn't have any wiggle room if he didn't want to feel the strain of the ropes. I was keeping an eye on his limbs to make sure their color looked right and there was no swelling. I wasn't sure that Eamon could answer truthfully, and we didn't know each other well enough for me to be able to ensure he knew his limits.

I slapped his ass. "I will stop if you keep talking."

He whimpered, making me feel powerful. God, he was beautiful. This man was my fantasy come to life. I needed to get inside him.

I walked over to the small table near the wall that held supplies, choosing first a few packets of lube and then ripping open a condom and putting it on.

"Are you ready for my cock, you slut? I bet you've had hundreds of cocks up that sloppy ass, coming inside you until you're full and it drips out all day long. Do you want me to open the door so everyone can see how much you like to be bent over? Everyone can come and take a turn."

He shuddered, and if I didn't fuck him soon, I was going to come before I got inside him. I planned to mix it up a little. I ripped one of the packets of lube open with my teeth and squeezed some onto my fingers. I circled his pink puckered hole slowly for him to get used to having someone touch him there. Once he started to relax, I stuck one finger in, trying to loosen him up. He was fucking tight, and the thought of that hole squeezing the hell out of my cock was making me sweat. I moved my finger around until I found the spongy area of his prostate.

"Ah, oh." He tried to move to keep feeling my finger on his prostate, but I was deliberately circling on and off the area to drive him mad. I stuck two fingers in and started to scissor them. I knew he would like a little pain. He needed to be stretched just enough.

"You filthy slut, you could take my whole fist and have room for more."

By the time I had managed three fingers, I was ready to burst. I got the lube and added some to my cock, then pulled my fingers out and rammed my cock inside him.

"Fuck, Jarrod!" he screamed.

"You know what you have to do to make this stop." I was struggling to get words together, he felt so divine.

"No!" That was screamed louder than my name.

Thank fuck, because I didn't want to stop. An ass had never felt this good before. Seeing him tied up and at my mercy was what dreams were made of.

I was deliberately avoiding his prostate, and the cock ring was doing its job, stopping him from coming.

"How do you like a big juicy cock pounding your ass?" I wanted to hear him as I reduced him to a drooling mess.

"Jarrod, let me come, please." His voice was whiny and desperate.

"Bad boys don't come unless I say they can. I could keep you like this for hours. Why don't you beg me to hit your prostate?"

"Please, Sir," he said in a timid and soft tone I hadn't thought him capable of.

"Maggot, that was pathetic. Yell, cry, and make me believe you want it."

He was nearly sobbing with need. "Sir, please give me your big cock and make me come. I beg you, I need it!" he yelled, the decibels high.

Fuck, I missed a stroke and nearly fell on top of him. I pulled out, needing to calm down or this would be over too quickly. I got back into place and adjusted my angle, which wasn't easy with the height of the chair and Eamon being in a fixed position. I entered slowly, and I knew I had hit the mark when Eamon tensed all of his muscles. His hole clamped down on my cock, making me see stars. Nothing had been this tight on my cock before.

Eamon let out a shuddering moan. I was pounding his prostate and he had nowhere to go. I was done. He felt too good and I couldn't keep going. I reached around and pulled off the cock ring, throwing it to the floor.

Eamon arched his back as much as he could in the ropes. "Sir, I'm coming," he screamed.

I let it be. I was caught up in my own arousal and I just needed to come before I exploded.

He let out a wail and came, his channel squeezing the life out of me. That was it—I came with a guttural roar. Cum filled up the condom as I emptied my balls. We were both panting like we had run a marathon. For me, it was the most intense sexual experience of my life. I needed a few seconds to catch my breath before untying Eamon. I wasn't sure of his reaction. I hoped he'd allow me to give him aftercare.

I was in my head. Jarrod, get it together. The ropes had been on for a while now and needed to be released. I pulled out of Eamon, tied off the condom, and threw it on the table. I would collect that when we packed up. I didn't want to leave any of my DNA around in such an obvious place. I gave myself a mental shake to get my head in the game and stepped back over to Eamon, then started to untie the ropes. He had beads of sweat all over his body, and I wanted to follow them with my tongue as they rolled down his spine. I had to stop these thoughts. The scene was over and he was my enemy.

Once the ropes were undone, I spun him around and pushed him to sit in the chair. He needed the blood to flow back to his limbs properly, and until that happened, he would experience pins and needles. His head was down as he looked at the floor. For him, this must have been mind-blowing. These types of scenes could be very overwhelming.

I grabbed two bottles of water from the table, handing one over to Eamon.

He whispered, "thanks."

I got the aloe vera lotion and spread it on his back. If this was intense for me, it would take him a while to be able to function.

I crouched down in front of him and put my hands on his knees. There was a slight tensing of his muscles, but I kept my hands there so he felt some connection to another person.

"Are you okay? Are you having any difficulty with your arms or legs?"

He raised his eyes and I felt like I could see into his soul. There was this aura of sadness that clung to him like a shield. In this moment, it was hard to imagine this man was a killer. I was seeing something that no one on the planet would have seen. I hope it didn't get me killed because this man couldn't afford to be weak. Anyone who saw this and knew who he was wouldn't live to see the next sunset.

"Everything is fine. It was a great scene, thank you," he said in a monotone voice.

He was shedding the submissive Eamon and taking back his control. I stood up and got dressed, then handed his clothes to him. While he dressed, I cleaned up and untangled my ropes. All this was done in awkward silence. Once I was done, I looked over at Eamon to find him staring at me. It was like a silent acknowledgment that something profound had happened in this room that changed both of us. I gave a small nod and we headed to the door. I was closest, and when I pulled the door open, the humidity hit us in the face. We had been in air-conditioned comfort, which I was grateful for considering how much we'd both sweated anyway. We headed in the same direction toward our rooms. I needed a nap after the emotionally draining scene we had just done.

From the corner of my eye, I saw a reflection of bright sunlight off a weapon. I was trained to notice even the smallest hint of danger.

"Down, now." I didn't think, just reacted, crashing into Eamon and bringing him to the ground. The person was using a silencer, but when the bullets hit the planter boxes and the metal support beams for the awning, they made a lot of noise. We crab walked back behind a row of horizontal planters to give us better coverage, then looked at each other as if to say what now? We'd been stupid and complacent. Neither of us had brought guns to the scene, knowing we'd have to undress. These types of mistakes got you killed.

"Do you have any idea why someone would be shooting at us?" Eamon said, eyebrows raised. The shots stopped for now, but that didn't mean whoever it was wouldn't rush our hiding spot. We had no idea how many people were targeting us.

I wanted to rant and rave, but the truth was I didn't know who the target was. The shots were fired at both of us. I had plenty of enemies, and my father would not approve of why I was here. And yes, he would shoot me and not lose a minute's sleep.

"No, I was thinking the same of you." We glared at each other, knowing that both of us were hiding something.

We were both full of shit, and we were going to have to work together to get out of this situation alive. The fucking irony was not lost on me!

Chapter 11

Eamon

The first time I wasn't packing, some asshole decided to shoot at me. Even more interesting? Jarrod was not acting like a civilian who was pinned down by someone firing at us. He was the one who had noticed the threat a split second before me. It wouldn't be a stretch to say that he might have saved our lives.

What I couldn't work out was why the shooter was targeting both of us. There was a good reason for a gun to be in my face, but I was starting to think Jarrod had secrets I needed to dig into because this scenario was ringing a lot of alarm bells.

"Eamon, we need to move. They know we aren't armed and are going to ambush us."

He was right. We needed to make a run for the thick foliage that was just behind the cottage we were crouched beside. Our only hope was to generate an element of surprise where we could take the upper hand with hand-to-hand combat. To do that, we needed to find a hiding spot and be patient, letting our attacker come to us.

We were both fit and liked to run, so we should be able to outpace them. The dangerous part would be once we jumped up and moved away from our cover, as well as the few short steps we had to take before the lush forest could swallow us up.

I was closer to the exit point, so I would need to go first. I hated the idea that Jarrod was at my back. For all I knew, these people could be with him, and this could be a ruse to separate me from the more populated resort area. I assessed all the available options, and I had no choice but to trust Jarrod for now. I would reassess my options as we went along. This was not how I'd envisaged the end of my sexual fantasy. I was pissed that I couldn't even have this moment in time to live the way I wanted to and enjoy the afterglow.

He dropped his bag of equipment he brought to our scene and left it behind the planter box. "One, two, three," Jarrod said softly.

I was up like I had springs attached to my feet. Jarrod was so close behind me I could feel his breath as he disturbed the humid air. I heard a few shots fired but I didn't stop. I was sure nothing had hit me, and Jarrod was still behind me, keeping up with the pace I set.

As we ran past trees, branches hit us in the face and moisture collected from the overnight rain sprayed all over our clothes. There was one hurdle we had to navigate, the twelve foot fences around the resort. The fence itself was shielded by foliage, which helped us stay covered. When we got there, I launched myself up and caught the top crossbar in my hands, using the momentum to get my leg up and over to balance on top. I put my hand down for Jarrod. He grabbed mine and I lifted him up, and then we both jumped down on the other side. We didn't have time to have a nice stroll and avoid the denser part of the undergrowth, so we just cut through the foliage that was in front of us.

I had automatically gone in a zigzag formation, using the larger trees as silent protectors. Once we were enough distance away and I couldn't hear any pursuit, I slowed down and then came to a stop. The next part we would do by stealth to help cover our mad dash through the forest. Jarrod was quiet like a mouse, able to walk through the forest quietly and not leave a mark, which required extensive training. Something wasn't right here, and I needed to get to the bottom of it.

We both nodded to the same tree to climb, another glaring clue he'd had training. The tree had two thick branches that spread wide, allowing us to both be high and cover all the directions that our enemy might come from. We got into position easily, and I could only hear the sounds of the forest—birds tweeting, the buzzing of insects, and the rustling of small animals in the underbrush. Under the canopy of the trees, the air was still and the humidity higher without any sea breeze.

I looked at Jarrod, and I was sure he could feel the heat of my stare. "You're not who you say you are," I whispered.

He looked over at me. "Neither are you."

It wasn't long before we heard someone crashing through the forest. They obviously didn't go to the same school of stealth that it seemed Jarrod and I went to. The problem was I now heard others approaching from behind us, meaning we would be bringing our fists to a gunfight and be outnumbered.

Jarrod and I eyeballed each other. "Fight or flight?" I asked.

Jarrod wiped the sweat off his forehead. "I don't think we're going to get the option of flight."

I noticed blood on his arm. "Were you hit?"

"Just a flesh wound."

He ripped the bottom of his shirt to make a temporary bandage. At least he knew that the bigger risk was the microbes in this forest that could infect the wound and he covered it up.

"The plan?" I asked. I had a feeling he was a soldier—or at least trained in combat.

He shrugged. "You take the front and I take the back?"

I didn't know what to say to that. I must be hearing sexual innuendo in everything that came out of that sexy mouth.

If I was going to die, I would go out with a bang. I smiled at him. "I liked your cock."

He gave me a cheeky grin. "I loved fucking your hole."

"If we live through this, let's have an encore," I said.

He saluted me, and then five men were under our tree. I swung down, leaving my hands on the branch to kick one in the head as hard as I could. Running shoes weren't as good as my ass-kicking boots, but beggars couldn't be choosers. I was able to smash his nose in, and he thumped to the ground like a felled log in the forest. The fighting was fierce, and they got a few good hits to my face and body, but I gave as good as I got. Until I felt a sting in my neck and reached up and pulled out a dart.

"Oh fuck," Jarrod said. Two men had him restrained by the arms, and another had an arm around Jarrod's neck, holding him in place.

He wouldn't like being restrained as much as me. Would we get tied up? My eyesight was getting foggy, and for some reason I wanted to lie down. I fell to the ground on my knees and then fell forward, face down. For me it was lights out.

Sometime later I started to regain consciousness. I left my eyes closed to gauge where I was and how much danger I was in. I was sitting in what felt like a wooden chair and my hands were tied behind my back, with my feet tied to the legs of the chair. It smelled dank and moist, like a moldy basement that had been left to rot. I was sweating profusely from the humidity. It made me think we hadn't been taken off the island.

I slowly opened my eyes to a slit to view the room and saw Jarrod was tied up beside me. The rest of the room was empty of people and furniture. It was more of a wooden shack in the forest. Some of the plant life was growing through the joints in the wood, the only light filtering into the room coming through those very small gaps. The floor was uneven, like the foundations had given up. I had no idea what this had been used for, but it now looked like it was abandoned.

Jarrod was slumped in his chair on my right with his head hanging forward. I felt guilty that my business had dragged him into this mess, but something wasn't right here. He wasn't just another guy on vacation. I would bet my life on it, and it might come to that.

"Jarrod, wake up." I kept my voice low, just in case there were guards posted outside the shack who might hear me speaking.

Jarrod showed signs of waking. He shook his head and turned to me with sleepy eyes. I could see his spatial awareness kick in as he took in our current location and situation.

"How long have you been awake?" Jarrod said.

"Not long, only minutes. When I woke, we were like this, and I haven't seen anyone."

My mouth was so dry, I would have killed for an ice-cold water. A nice dip in the pool would work as well. Somehow, I didn't think these new accommodations would have either of those things.

Jarrod cringed and looked away like he had something to hide.

I narrowed my eyes at him. "This is not the time for bullshit. If you know something, you need to tell me. We need to put everything on the table to get out of this alive."

He stared at me, and I could tell he was weighing his options. "Okay, but you're hiding secrets too. I'll tell you my truth, but I want to know something about someone close to me. Do you promise to tell me the truth, even if it relates to Velatus Deus?"

What the fuck? How did he know that name? I couldn't afford to play games, and it seemed that this situation was crossing over into my world. I was tied up and I had nothing to lose at this point, so I would give him what he wanted.

"Agreed." I had to get out of here, and I'd probably need his help to make that happen.

He nodded and took a deep breath. "I recognized some of the goons. They work for my father."

This was getting interesting. "Who is your father?"

Jarrod sighed loudly. "My sperm donor's name is Conrad Sawtell."

Shock hit me right between the eyes. Conrad was a senior member of Velatus Deus, but I had never trusted the bastard and had been watching him for some time.

"I'm not sure where you sit on the scale of Conrad being evil versus being a great guy, but I can tell you he is the scum of the earth, and as soon as I was eighteen, I disappeared. Being related to him does not mean a thing, and he isn't loyal to anyone, including the Velatus Deus."

Conrad had the full resources of the Velatus Deus at his disposal. I would have thought disappearing from someone in the Velatus Deus would be impossible, unless you went off the grid, and even then I would have my doubts.

Jarrod smiled at me, and I was reminded of how handsome he was. "I can see you have doubts that it's possible. Of course he found me, but I had set myself up with the Byrne mercenary group that you partner with, and they protected me. Daddy was told if anything happened to me, he would be the next one they went after. Don't think he didn't try, but those he sent just weren't as good as me."

That made sense. Velatus Deus would be all over Conrad's ass if he fucked up the working arrangement with the Byrne mercenaries. We also would have looked into him harder, which he wouldn't have wanted. Byrne's people were hardcore, and no one wanted to be on their hit list. That meant that Jarrod was in elite company and a badass in his own right or he wouldn't have made it into the group.

Fuck my life, had I been sleeping with the enemy? Why was he here? And I'd let him tie me up. Why did finding out how dangerous Jarrod was get me horny? *I must have a death wish!*

Chapter 12

Jarrod

I had no choice but to trust Eamon. The *enemy of my enemy is my friend* sort of thing. I was hoping that Eamon would tell me what he knew.

"I want to know what happened to my brother." I didn't know how much time we had before someone came back to this shit shack.

Eamon frowned. "Your brother was Kayd Sawtell?"

I nodded, having difficulty swallowing from the lump in my throat. I coughed to get air in and then I could speak again. Talking about my brother still made me come undone.

"Kayd was eight years younger than me and we had different mothers. Conrad stayed with Kayd's mother and treated him differently than me. In some ways, he became the heir, especially after he went into the family business. We kept in touch on the side, and I think Conrad knew but let it go. About eight months ago, Kayd messaged he was undercover but something wasn't right and he needed to go silent for a while. I got a quick message six weeks later that basically said there were traitors and he needed to find out who they were. Two months later he was declared dead. I didn't trust Conrad one bit, so I broke into the funeral home the night before the funeral to see who was there ready to be buried."

I had to collect myself. Until that night, I hadn't believed that Kayd was dead and had been hoping for it to be a mistake. I'd thought maybe our father was lying and they were burying someone else. I took a deep breath.

"It was Kayd, and he was definitely dead."

I drilled my eyes into Eamon. He'd had many years to learn how to hide his emotions, so I knew he wasn't going to break down and spill all of Velatus Deus's secrets.

His eyes widened. "Jarrod, I was told that Kayd died in the field. I read the report provided by all agents involved and our intelligence team. Something about that mission and what we were doing did cause doubts in my mind, but it was more intuitive than fact. When the senior operator signed off, I let it be."

I was getting somewhere. I needed to know who was involved. "Who signed off on it?"

"Your father."

Was this him all along? My stomach clenched. Father would protect himself first, even over his own child. I was starting to get a bad feeling that my enemy was closer to me than I'd thought all this time.

The door burst open and bright light hit us, making both of us shut our eyes from the extreme change from dark to light. My father walked in like the villain he was, dressed like an actor in a black-and-white movie.

"Hello, boys. Nice to see you both."

I rolled my eyes. Was this a dream or a nightmare? "Hello, Father. Fancy seeing you here." I wasn't even surprised anymore. This man was evil to the core.

"Jarrod, yes, imagine my surprise when I followed Eamon and I found you here as well. Not only that, but both of you were without your security entourage. Did you need to make it so easy for me?"

He was so excited, I thought he might break out in song and tap dance across the floor. He turned away from me and stood in front of Eamon. In the doorway, there were two goons dressed in black tactical pants and t-shirts. My father was still in a suit, even in this heat. Nothing screamed organized crime family cliché more than a dude in a suit with his own security dressed in fatigues on a tropical island filled with bikinis.

"This is quite the place. I think I might come back and have a vacation here. A place called Leather Persuasion sounds like just the thing to spice up my life."

Since many people walked around the resort naked, I really didn't need that image in my mind before I died.

I thought of my brother and my anger came back with a vengeance. "So, this is a coup then? How does Kayd fit into this picture?"

Father lost the smirk that had been on his face since he'd arrived and his eyes narrowed. I knew then it was him all along. I could see it in his eyes. Eamon had told the truth, and all the pieces were falling into place.

"It was you. How could you kill your own son?" I yelled. I wanted to cry. This bastard had taken from me the only person on this earth I loved.

He stopped walking around in front of us and frowned. There was an awkward silence where all I could hear was animals rustling in the underbrush and birds chirping and calling to each other. I kept working on my ropes. This bastard was going to kill us, family or not.

"He was not loyal to me. When he found out my plans, he was going directly to him!" he screamed, pointing at Eamon. The crazy was bleeding into his eyes. "I had no choice. Kayd picked his side, and like you, he didn't pick his family."

He started clapping, the noise abrupt and jarring. "That was in the past. I'm going to build a new dynasty and direction for the Velatus Deus, and both of you need to disappear for that to happen. The good news is that no one knows where either of you are. You're both booked under fake names. I can throw you in the water for the sharks and no one will be the wiser."

He laughed, and it had a manic tone to it. Out of the corner of my eye, I saw that Eamon was working on the ropes on his hands. He was an expert, and I bet he had taught himself how to get out of them just in case a scene went bad. Was being tied up making him hard? *Fuck, Jarrod. We're about to be murdered and you're thinking about Eamon's cock!* To be fair, it was a great-looking cock. I think the heat had fried my brain.

My ropes were loosening. Eamon gave me a sideways look, and I knew he was ready. I hoped we weren't just bringing fists to a gunfight. Father had moved back behind his two goons—a sign they were going to shoot us. We had run out of time, and it was now or never. Eamon exploded out of his chair. His legs were still tied to the legs, and he used brute force to break the wood so he could move. I had loosened my ropes enough to be able to get to my feet with the chair on my back. I faced away from the goons and ran backward, using the chair as the weapon.

A gunshot went off near me but I didn't feel any pain. I hoped Eamon was still fighting on and it hadn't distracted him. I kept swinging the chair backward and forward, hoping to hit someone.

I felt a hand on my arm just as I was about to do a one-eighty.

"Jarrod, it's me. I'm cutting your ropes," Eamon said.

The chair crashed to the floor and the ropes were next. My hands and feet tingled as the circulation started to come back. My father and his goons were knocked out on the floor.

I grinned at Eamon. "You want those ropes for souvenirs?" Eamon rolled his eyes. "What, too soon?" That earned me a smirk.

"Come on. We need to get out of here and see where we are," Eamon said.

"Did you get shot?" I asked him.

"Nah, these idiots couldn't hit the broad side of a barn even when standing a foot away."

I gave him a genuine smile. Now I knew he had nothing to do with my brother's death, I was allowing myself to look my fill and not feel guilty about it.

I grabbed the gun off the floor, and it only had three bullets in it. What sort of a bad guy was this, to have a gun that wasn't even fully loaded? There'd only been one shot fired. These guys were not Velatus Deus. There was no way they would have passed the extensive training.

I walked over to my father with the gun in my hand. I wanted to blow his brains out. Eamon came up behind me and circled his arms around my chest. I rested my head on his shoulder.

"Now is not the time. We don't want bodies to be found, and we are also unaccounted for. Their time will come. We need to get out of here," Eamon said.

I knew he was right. I just wanted this chapter of my life—where I got justice for Kayd—to be over, and then I could move on from this obsession. I might be replacing that obsession with a new one. Eamon walked over to some bags in the corner that had been left by the goons and searched through them. I checked my wound. My makeshift bandage was holding, but blood was seeping through. I needed it cleaned properly as soon as possible, but it would have to do for now.

Watching Eamon was my new favorite pastime. Even dirty, sweaty, and smelly, he was gorgeous, and I wanted to fuck him again. My cock pointed north, which was a tad inconvenient, but I couldn't criticize my taste in men. Since I had fucked him, it was all I could think about. Curse these assholes for fucking up the moment.

Eamon looked up and caught me staring. He raised his eyebrows, and I shook my head. We needed to make tracks. I went to my father and kicked him in the head. It felt good mentally but now my toes hurt.

Eamon grabbed my hand and pulled me out the door. Hand holding felt intimate and, in some ways, very high school. In this case, it was about comfort. It wasn't every day your father tried to kill you and you found out he killed your brother. It sounded like a stupid movie plot.

Once we were outside, as I expected, we discovered this shack was in the middle of nowhere, and because of the dense trees and foliage, we couldn't see any landmarks or the ocean.

"Let's get away from here and then maybe climb a tree to see if we can recognize where we are," Eamon said.

"Sounds good." There wasn't any access for vehicles near here, but I doubted daddy dearest and the goons would have hiked too far. Still, we didn't know which direction they came from and it all looked the same. I was feeling a little sore around the ribcage, so I think the goons must of carried us here in a firemen's hold.

Eamon never let go of my hand as we walked. We were both fit, so we were able to make good time as we trekked through the jungle. I was starting to hate the smell of my armpits, though, and the hot, humid weather was doing a number on me. Eamon had found two bottles of water, but we were trying to conserve them just in case we had to stay overnight. Based on where the sun was, I would say it was late afternoon.

"Do you think it's the same day we were taken?" I asked.

"Yeah, I do. We would have been more dehydrated if we had been left in that hot shack for more than a day."

We were far enough away to be able to take a breath and get our bearings. Eamon climbed a tree and looked around. I looked down at my arm, and the temporary bandage was now dirty and blood soaked. My luck, I'd get a tropical disease and die from that, instead of from being shot by a substandard goon.

Eamon jumped down, then came over and put his hands on my shoulders. "Are you okay?"

"I guess. I didn't think it was him, but I should have. I knew he was capable of it. I wish Kayd had shared the burden with me and let me help him."

Eamon kissed me lightly on the mouth. "He'd been indoctrinated into Velatus Deus all his life and would have thought he could deal with it. As a good agent, he also would have wanted to be very sure before condemning his father. I think someone betrayed him at the end, and I'm going to find out who that was." He was back to being the leader. I pitied anyone who got in his way because heads were going to roll.

I stared up at him. "Thank you."

He squeezed my shoulders. "Come on, the beach is the way we are heading, and I'm pretty sure it's the same side of the island that the resort is on. We'll follow the forest line bordering the beach back to the resort."

We started up a slow jog. We were hungry and thirsty, but we could only fix that when we got back. Twenty minutes passed before we could see the beach. There was a small run downhill, and then we started running parallel to the water, but we were still within the cover of the trees.

"God, I wish I could just run into that water," I said.

"I don't think it's worth a bullet to the head."

I rolled my eyes. Party pooper. Still, he was right. There was too much open space here that someone could use to take us out.

We ran for another ten minutes before we could see the resort in the distance.

"Um... we should go to my room. I bugged yours," I said sheepishly.

He raised his eyebrows at me. "Maybe I bugged yours," he said, then he laughed. "The look on your face. I didn't bug your room, otherwise I would have known what you were up to."

"Well fuck, I'm glad. I would have missed out on that earth-moving sex we had, and I really want a chance to do that again."

I glanced at Eamon to see his reaction, hoping he felt the same. We had a connection, and if we could get out of this mess, I wanted to explore it.

"If you think you're going to get away from me now that I've found you, think again."

We shared a smile. Finding someone who shared your same sexual preferences and also knew about your super-secret society would be rare. I was like a fucking unicorn.

We were approaching the outer buildings of the resort, and we needed to cross in front of a few general-purpose rooms to get to my cottage. I looked across the lawn and spotted Lance, who noticed us as well and started walking our way.

He looked us up and down and screwed up his nose. "What the hell happened to you both. Is that blood on Jarrod's arm?"

Eamon stepped up. "We went for a walk and I tripped and took Jarrod with me. It's just a scratch, I will clean it up when we get back to our rooms." He smiled cheekily. "You know how that might have ended."

Lance smirked. "Ah well, a few clothes were killed in the process, but I'm sure you had fun."

Eamon reached back and grabbed my hand. "Now I need a nice long shower and a man to cuddle."

Lance giggled. "I won't keep you then."

We doubled-timed it back to my room. As long as only our clothes were killed and not us, I'd still classify this as a good day.

Chapter 13

Eamon

Luckily Jarrod still had his key in his pocket. Mine had been lost along the way somewhere. Once we were inside Jarrod's room and we knew it was safe, I grabbed him and pushed him back against the door, using my thumb to wipe away some of the dirt on his cheek. I slowly moved my head down so he had time to pull away, and then I kissed him with all the pent-up sexual tension I had inside me. It quickly turned hot and heavy, our tongues dueling, and I licked the inside of his mouth. I wanted to taste every part of him, but now wasn't the time.

"I wish we had more time," I said.

He smiled at me. "We'll have time when this is over and VD isn't trying to kill us, and you'll owe me a real vacation."

I laughed. "VD? If we get out of this, I'll upgrade us to the top-tier room. How about that?"

He rolled his eyes. "Yeah, like a venereal disease. Whatever, money bags."

I shook my head and gave him a peck on the lips and let him go. I noticed the bandage on his arm was soaked in blood.

"Is the wound deep?" I hated seeing him hurt. It was making my stomach churn.

He looked down at his arm. "The bullet grazed me, but it's not deep and I don't need stitches."

My blood pressure rose. "Fuck, Jarrod. That was too close."

He patted me on the cheek. "I know, but we need to focus."

I took his word for it and left it for now. Our phones were taken but it didn't matter. Mine was a burner and I was sure Jarrod's was as well.

"Go take a shower. If we both get in there, I can't guarantee it will be fast. I'll start enacting the emergency protocols and let everyone know that Conrad is enemy number one."

I could see how this had shattered Jarrod, the betrayal stabbing him deep. That bastard was going to pay.

Jarrod nodded and went into the bathroom. I used the room phone to call our encrypted number and gave all the required passwords and Latin code words. The head of my intelligence team would call me back.

Jarrod wasn't even out of the shower when the phone rang. I answered and kept quiet. All the current passcodes and sentences were given correctly.

"Simon," I said.

"What the hell is going on, Eamon?"

I'd always liked this guy. I hoped he wasn't involved, but I had also invoked a backup plan just in case.

"Conrad Sawtell is trying to kill me."

"What? Are you sure?"

"As sure as I can be when he had a gun pointed at me," I said sarcastically.

"Fucking hell."

I gave him my location, letting him know I wanted troops on the ground ASAP. Jarrod came out of the bathroom toweling his hair.

"Simon, I want you to pull everything you can find on the Kayd Sawtell matter, and I mean everything. Anyone standing in the way will be considered my enemy at this point."

Simon let out a sigh. "Has it come to that then?"

"Yes, and I plan on cleaning house. You're either with me or against me, and I'll be dealing with everyone who is my enemy with extreme prejudice. I hope I've made myself clear."

"Crystal."

"Good. Also, Jarrod Sawtell is considered to have the highest clearance, and he is to be protected at all costs."

"Okay."

"Simon, don't let me down. Let all the heads know to expect trouble from inside the organization."

"I won't let you down, I promise."

I ended the call, then looked at Jarrod, who just had a towel around his hips. I licked my lips before I could stop myself and got a lazy smile back from him.

"Call Byrne so he knows you're safe and that you're with me. I don't know who is compromised, so I'm bringing them in as well."

I left him to it and headed to the bathroom. When the water hit me, it felt like heaven. My back was still really sore. I tried not to think about why that was or I would pop a boner, and now was not the time. Once I got out, I used the spare towel to dry off, then wrapped it around me and walked into the room.

"Do you have some clothes I can wear?"

Jarrod was just wearing shorts. He'd removed the bandage on his arm, and I could see the graze. He was right, it wasn't deep—infection was the greatest risk from the wound getting dirty.

Picking up some boxer briefs and jogging shorts, he walked over to stand in front of me. He ran the flat of his hand down my chest all the way to my happy trail, and I pulled him to me and kissed him. I knew this wasn't the time, but I just had to taste his lips again.

"This isn't over between us. You don't have what we've shared with just anyone. I want to explore where we can take this."

He gave me a sexy grin. "Big guy, if you think you're getting away from me, you can think again. Our story hasn't been told yet."

We smiled at each other. It was an untold promise we made, but first we needed to kill some traitors.

As I dressed, Jarrod went to his bag, pulled out a new phone, and got it ready. Once he had it together, he sat at the end of the bed and called Byrne, putting it on speaker when it connected.

"What the fuck are you doing playing house with VD?" Byrne said.

We both laughed. Byrne never held back, and you got the hard truth whether you wanted it or not.

"I'll give you the short answer. I came to fuck Eamon up but got screwed over by Conrad, who got lucky and kidnapped us both. We escaped and now we're trapped on an island with him and his traitorous soldiers, who are trying to implement a coup. Oh, and Conrad killed my brother because Kayd found out what our father was up to."

When Jarrod got to the last bit, his voice hitched. I sat beside him and placed my arm around his shoulders, and he rested his head on my pec.

"Fuck my life, boys. You know how to create an action-packed vacation. As soon as I heard from Eamon's guy, I had troops moving. I have some nearby and they're going to helicopter in. We'll try for stealth, but I can't guarantee it, so be prepared for some fallout just in case. ETA will be three hours, so stay the fuck alive until then. Oh, and Eamon? Jarrod is like a son to me. I'll kill you if you let him die."

Byrne abruptly disconnected the call.

I looked at Jarrod and he grinned. "Yeah, the grumpy bastard is more of a father than that piece of shit out there. I have a hacker friend I need to call. We need to move to a vacant room, just in case."

I nodded because it was a good idea.

He called another number. "It's me," he said when someone answered on the other end.

"Where the fuck have you been? I've been worried sick."

"Ben, I'm fine, but I need you to find a cottage near mine that is empty."

"Fine, but I want the story later."

"You got it."

"The cottage three down from you, 302, is vacant."

"Okay. I have to go, but I'll check in tomorrow when I'm in a secure situation, I promise."

"Make sure you do." The line went dead.

I raised my eyebrows at Jarrod. Who was this person he'd taken direction from?

"Don't look like that. Ben and I have been friends since middle school and we work together. He's an independent contractor, if you will."

As he spoke, he packed up his bag and fired up his laptop. "I have a few cameras outside. I'm going to check if anyone is casing the room."

While I'd thought I was having an incognito vacation, in reality, I was being spied on and measured up. If it had been anyone else but Jarrod, I would have been dead on the first day. It was a sobering thought.

"I can't see any movement. Let's make a dash to your cottage and then get to 302."

Jarrod went first, which I wasn't happy about, but he was at the door quicker. He opened it slowly. When no shots were fired, we exited fast, running to my cottage. It didn't take me long to gather the few belongings that were outside my bag. The best part? I was now armed and I could set up my own burner phone. When we got to cottage 302, we used the master key that Jarrod had stolen. The cottage was smaller and set back from the others and had a restricted view of the ocean. The resort probably only used it when they were full.

I messaged my contacts my new number and waited for intelligence to come back. Velatus Deus was worldwide, and Conrad could have his claws all over our network. I had to make sure he was stopped at every angle.

Jarrod was fussing around in his bags. I walked over and pulled him to me, wrapping him in my arms. He felt like he had always been there. We agreed that one of us needed to stay awake, so we would do two-hour stints, where one of us slept while the other stood guard. I convinced him to sleep first so I could check in with my contacts.

This man was becoming important to me, and I needed to protect him. Today had been emotionally draining. It started with the best sexual experience of my life and ended with betrayal and us on the run, hunted like rabbits!

Chapter 14

Jarrod

Eamon and I worked well together. I sat here, watching him sleep. Would he think that was creepy? We had heard from Byrne's people. Because we were safe, they were going to hunt Father and his minions. The terrain around here was difficult once you got away from the coastal areas. Byrne had sent over two of his best trackers, saying it wouldn't be hard for them because they were used to working in jungles.

I was all twisted up about Eamon. He brought out feelings in me that I hadn't thought I was capable of. Once I knew he'd had nothing to do with Kayd's death, my walls came down and I allowed myself to feel. I could see what was happening between us, but I didn't think I could just welcome Velatus Deus with open arms. My hatred for the organization and my father had festered for many years.

Night had fallen and it heightened my sense of dread that something would be waiting to take us out. My laptop pinged. Something or someone had tripped my cameras. I grabbed it and sat at the small desk, then logged into my surveillance system. The camera facing my original cottage's patio door had been triggered as someone quietly tried to break into my room. They were wearing all black, including having their face covered.

"Eamon, wake up."

He sat up straight away and came to stand behind me. "Someone is trying to break into my cottage, and I'm wondering if they are breaking into your room as well." I split the screen in half and had pictures of each of our rooms side by side.

We didn't know if anyone knew we were in this room. We got our weapons ready and packed our extra clips into the pockets of our cargo shorts. We were already dressed and had shoes on—we'd been sleeping like that just in case we had to make a run for it.

The camera feeds from both of our cottages showed that there were two assassins, one in each separate cottage, and they had realized we weren't there. There wasn't even anything to search because we had all our property with us.

Out of nowhere, other assassins walked up behind our two room invaders and snapped their necks. That wasn't as easy as it looked—you needed to get the exact right place and have the brute strength to do it, all in one movement.

The new assassins made hand signals around the rooms at each of the walls.

"What the hell was that?" Eamon said, frowning.

I smiled. "That was Byrne's elite assassins taking out the trash."

"How the fuck do you know who it was?"

I laughed. The assassins did look stupid flopping around the room doing interpretive dance. "Basically, because they just told me."

I was fucking with Eamon. I had secret squirrel business as well, and I couldn't help but tease him.

I smirked. "We all get encrypted messages every twenty-four hours. I just checked and those were the hand signals for this twenty-four-hour cycle. They must have been told I had cameras, but they didn't know where they were so that's why they did the signals facing each wall."

We both jumped when we heard gunfire. It wasn't over the cameras and mic, but it wasn't far from the door of our current room. We threw ourselves onto the floor, side by side. I could feel the heat from Eamon's body. Now was not the time to think about his cock.

The door wasn't that thick, and if the bad guys were using high-caliber guns, then it would go straight through. The gunfire lasted about twenty seconds. There was no way they were going to explain this away as fireworks or some other type of sound because it was too distinctive.

We stayed where we were for thirty minutes and none of our phones rang, so intel was not forthcoming. As we lay there, we didn't even know if the good guys were winning.

Finally, my phone buzzed with an incoming call, and it was Byrne. I answered.

"Boys, you can stop lying around blowing each other while we do all the work. Come help us get rid of the bodies," Byrne said.

We sat up.

"Jarrod, one of them is your father," Byrne said in a gruff voice.

"Okay." It was a bit anticlimactic. The bastard had threatened to kill us and now he was the one dead without me even lifting a finger. Was I supposed to feel sad? I didn't have any feelings about him. Once I knew he had killed my brother, he was dead to me. All that had been on my mind was stopping his breathing permanently.

"I have Jaime standing near your block of rooms to escort you to us." Byrne abruptly ended the call.

I stood up and Eamon followed. He pulled me into his arms. "Just because he was an asshole, it doesn't mean you can't grieve. He was the last of your family. You could also grieve for the father you wish you'd had."

He totally got me. My father had killed my brother—the person most precious to me—and at the same time, I wished that it could have been different and I'd had a normal father. No matter what the result of today had been, nothing different would have ever happened because he'd been a disgusting human being who'd needed to die. That was the best outcome today for me and the man in my arms.

I squeezed Eamon. "Thank you."

He kissed me lightly on the lips. The kiss was gentle and loving—not something we had been to each other so far, but it felt right.

"Come on, or Byrne, the bastard, will call us princesses in our tower, waiting to be rescued."

I laughed. "The asshole so would."

We geared up and left the room, leaving our stuff here for now. As soon as we stepped outside, Jaime walked up to me and gave me a man hug.

"Good to see you, Jarrod. It's been a while."

"You too, Jaime."

Eamon was frowning and staring at Jaime like he would put a bullet in his brain.

I grabbed hold of Eamon's arm. "Jaime, this is Eamon."

Jaime nodded. "Nice to meet you."

"Sure." I rolled my eyes at him.

Jaime turned and walked back into the trees. Even though it was night, it was still humid, and I started to sweat as soon as we picked up the pace and headed away from the resort. We traveled for about twenty minutes before we came upon the group from Byrne, and the old bastard himself stood in the middle of them all.

"About time you got off your ass. Or were you tied up and gagged?"

I stuck my middle finger up at him. What Eamon and I did in the bedroom stayed between us unless we agreed to let anyone know about it. "Fuck off, old man. What the hell are you doing here?"

He had a huge smile, showing a lot of teeth. "I was in Miami and my baby bird needed rescuing from the big bad Latin-loving freak show. Oh, Eamon. Sorry, I didn't see you."

I rolled my eyes, then went over and hugged him. Byrne hated thanks and emotions, which is why all the dad jokes to deflect, but him being here told everyone that I was family. He didn't do much fieldwork anymore.

"Okay, stop the touchy-feely stuff. Save that for your man over there who is staring lasers into all of us."

"Shut it, old man."

"Now that you're here, we can get cracking. We have bodies we need to get to a clearing that's a ten-minute walk away, and then we're going to basket them up to the chopper."

Byrne grabbed my arm. "While they get ready, do you want to see your father?"

"Yeah, I want closure."

I followed Byrne. I could sense Eamon walking up behind me. Father had been separated and left by himself in the grass. I wanted to see that he was dead. Otherwise,

I might have dreams of him somehow being resurrected—like in a B-grade movie—and continuing to fuck up my life. I found him lying there with a neat bullet hole in his forehead. He'd been sniped from a distance to get such a neat hole without the explosion of brain matter like there would have been from a close shot. Byrne left us there. Eamon wrapped his arms around my chest and pulled me back against him. It felt nice to be able to lean on someone. I had spent enough time on this asshole. He was gone, and Kayd's killer was now dead. It was time to move on.

I turned in Eamon's arms so I was facing him. "Okay, let's get this shitshow over with so we can finish the rest of our vacation."

"You want to stay here?" Eamon asked, surprised.

"Some of the best days of my life have been spent here. Also some of the most fucked up. I want the great days to totally outweigh those and get rid of them from my memory." I raised my eyebrows at Eamon. "We have a lot of exploring to do, and don't forget the fucking."

Eamon's eyes filled with lust. "Yes, Sir."

Fuck, my dick got hard in the weirdest places. I had all the time in the world to take my therapy out on Eamon's ass!

Chapter 15

Eamon

The bodies were all flown away. I didn't ask where, as long as they weren't found on the island. It would look like a massacre and have the press climbing all over the place. We went back to our temporary room, packed our things, and then headed back to Jarrod's room to get a few hours of sleep.

We slept in the same bed, with me being the big spoon. I thought it would be awkward to sleep beside someone, but I found it comforting. Jarrod made me feel like we had known each other for years instead of days. Now that I was awake, I wanted to stay with Jarrod in my arms, but my bladder was telling me I needed to get up.

Jarrod started to stretch and then he spun in my arms and laid his head on my pec with his eyes still closed. "Starving and need to pee."

I laughed and kissed him on the forehead. "Let's get up, and if we hurry, we can still make breakfast."

We did what we needed to and dressed. Breakfast would be over in fifteen minutes, so we fast walked to the dining room. We filled our plates, sat at a spare table, and ate like it was an Olympic event.

Lance wandered over after speaking to some guests, grinning at us. "Boys, you sure have worked up an appetite. The humid air is keeping you hot, sweaty, and energetic by the looks of things."

I glanced at Jarrod. If Lance knew what had been keeping us sweaty lately, we'd knock that permanent smile right off his face.

I wanted to forget yesterday and move on to something enjoyable. "Lance, is the Lotus Room available today and tomorrow?" I asked.

Jarrod's head whipped up, a piece of bacon still in his mouth. I grabbed it and stuck it in mine, and he snarled at me. I was sure I'd pay for that later.

Lance gave a polite cough. When I looked back at him, he wiggled his nose and smirked. "Well, the Lotus Room is free from one to four today and tomorrow. Would you like me to book it for you?"

"Yes, please." Jarrod gave me a big smile that made the hair on my arms stand on end. That smile was filled with dark delight, and I knew he was going to make me want to scream, though I probably wouldn't be able to make a sound.

"Fabulous. Did you hear about the local shoot-out that happened last night?"

Jarrod looked over at me. "No, we didn't," I said.

Lance sat down at our table. "Well, it was supposed to be hush-hush, but the local coast guard chased some real-life pirates and they came ashore here. Apparently, there was a little shoot-out and the bad guys went down. It happened in a flash and everyone was safe. Our security made sure that the resort and our guests were looked after. It sounded very exciting. Anyway, I must be off. Have a great afternoon. Toodles!" he said, then jumped up and quickly walked away.

Jarrod and I looked at each other and laughed. "Coast guard. Byrne will love that. I guess it's as good cover as any, what with the choppers being heard around the island. It definitely wasn't exciting on our end," Jarrod said. I nodded. That was the understatement of the year, being shot at and running through the jungle is not my type of good time.

No one could say that Leather Persuasion was boring. We still had two full days to explore before we had to head home, and I planned on enjoying every minute of it with Jarrod.

Jarrod stroked his chin with his fingers. "So, do we have plans, or did you book that room for you and someone else?"

I looked down my nose at him. "There is no one else but you in my eyes. I don't want there to be anyone else either."

Jarrod looked serious. I was starting to worry that he didn't feel the same about me.

"Eamon, I want to explore this with you, but I'm not sure I can take having Velatus Deus secret business around me after living through it with my father."

I didn't want this burden to take away something else from me. I couldn't have that be the only thing in my life. I had seen paradise, and I didn't want to go back to the shell of a life I was leading.

"There are no guarantees that we will work. I'm annoying as fuck and, until I came here, a workaholic. I want to change, and I want to bring VD to its knees before building it back up again."

I knew he would smile when I called it VD—it was his thing. His smile warmed me, and I hoped I could convince him to stay with me.

"Jarrod, we can do good out there, especially in the space of human trafficking. I'm proposing a partnership, not leaving you out, because that would never work for us. Will you help me steer this motherfucker around and use it to destroy the people who deserve it and be a voice for the victim?"

He stared at me, maybe measuring my words. "This is the first time I've seen you be so passionate about something," he said.

"Well, you've only known me for less than a week, but that's how I feel about you, too."

He hid a cough behind his fist. "Actually a lot longer than that. I spied on you for months."

I rolled my eyes. I should have known or suspected. He was good because I never caught him. I might need him to review my personal security.

He licked his lips slowly. "We still have two days, so why don't you convince me."

"Let's go for a swim and work off this breakfast, and then we have a date in the Lotus Room at one."

He gave me a big smile. "I like your plans, Eamon. You would have thought you were a top with that bossy energy," he cheekily said.

We stood up, and I moved to stand over him. "We'll see how much of a top you feel like when I'm squeezing the fuck out of your cock with my ass."

He bit his lip. "Did you have to give me a hard-on in the dining room just as we're about to leave?"

I turned toward the door that led outside and took a few steps before looking back. "Last one to the beach can suck cock for five minutes."

Our eyes met, and then it was a mad scramble to get out the door and down to the sand. I won, and Jarrod agreed to give me my prize later.

We swam and laughed and were openly affectionate with each other. Leather Persuasion Resort was a safe place to be yourself and indulge your sexuality.

When it was time, we went back to Jarrod's room and showered. I spent some time preparing for the afternoon activities. I was finding it hard to contain my excitement and act all nonchalant. As we walked to the Lotus Room, it was a whole different vibe from last time. Not only was there anticipation, but there was also the togetherness that had formed in a short time from our intense sexual connection and the trauma of being kidnapped. Nearly being killed by Conrad had also put things into perspective. Life was too short to live with regrets. My new motto was to grab life by the horns and make it my bitch.

Jarrod opened the door of the Lotus Room and ushered me in. My heart rate picked up. I knew once I was in this room, I was submissive Eamon with a pain and humiliation kink. The white Saint Andrew's cross dominated one side of the room. As soon as I entered and saw the equipment, all the blood rushed from my head to my cock. The room only had a table, couch, and two wooden chairs as far as furniture. The table held the floggers and a small box of smaller sexual equipment that was used once and then billed to your room. Like a good dominant, Jarrod inspected all the equipment and gave me a small nod confirming we were good to go. I undressed completely and Jarrod took off his shirt.

"Anything changed from our last scene about your limits?" Jarrod asked.

"No." Other then I knew how good it was going to be and how much I loved to be fucked by him.

"What is your safe word?"

"Virtus and answering to the traffic light system." Jarrod was serious about safety, and I was glad for it. I had gone too far once trying to use pain for sexual stimulation. I still bore the small scars from the knife play I'd engaged in and gone too far.

"Good. Let's get you strapped in."

I walked over to the cross, and Jarrod buckled the leather cuffs to my wrists. They were tight, but not enough to affect circulation. They were attached to chains that could be moved to adjust to different heights. My ankles were also cuffed.

Once I was strapped in facing the white cross, tingling started spreading all along my skin. Jarrod walked around in front of me, and he waited until I lifted my eyes to look at him.

"Eamon, you disgusting piece of shit," he snarled at me. "We put a little cuff on you, and you wiggle around like someone is stroking your cock, but that will not be happening and you will not come today unless I say so. Can you follow instructions, maggot?"

I knew not to talk unless he said I could. This was a way to get me to break and be a bad boy.

"I have a treat for you today, but I'm not sure you deserve it." His tone was sarcastic.

He pulled out from behind him some type of chain, and I realized it had clamps on each end. Jarrod attached the clamps to my nipples. The pain was instant and bolted through me. I had never engaged in nipple play before and I wasn't prepared for it.

"Have you done this before? You may speak."

"No." I was having trouble even getting my tongue to articulate any words.

Jarrod pulled on the chain.

"Ah." I couldn't help it. The pain and pleasure were electrifying me and dominating the little brain power I had.

He came up beside me and bit my earlobe, leaving a sting. "I'll let that go since this is your first time."

I felt Jarrod touch my dick. When I looked down, he had put a cock ring on me that also surrounded my balls and pulled them up. I was glad—it would help me not shoot too early.

I tried to keep my eyes open and not slip into the pleasure. Jarrod picked up the medium-sized flogger that he'd used last time, wasting no time walking to me and then whipping me with it. Every time I arched my back from the hits, it would make the clamps pull harder on my nipples. I was on a seesaw of pain that was making my legs feel like jelly.

"Eamon, what's your color?" I felt like I was at the other end of a long tunnel away from Jarrod. I needed to gather some brain cells to reply or he would stop.

"Green."

He started flogging me down my back again. I was surprised my cock didn't explode and send the cock ring flying across the room. I caught myself moaning. I'd had no idea I was making any noise.

Jarrod stopped and walked around to face me. "You're a fucking pain slut who will do anything for his next hit. Don't you have any dignity? Look at you. You're a dribbling mess."

My body was on fire and each twinge was sending me into rapture.

"Jarrod, I need to be fucked." I think he realized I was at my limit. If he gave me much more, I'd drift into subspace.

I was losing awareness. The next thing I felt was Jarrod's fingers up my ass, stretching me.

"I'm going to fuck this tight hole until I spray your insides with cum."

My cock and balls were tight and painful, throbbing to their own beat.

"Fuck. I love your ass, Eamon."

He pulled my cheeks apart and slammed his cock into me. The stretch burned until my hole was big enough to accommodate his size. His pounding was making the chain on the nipple clamps swing and pull my buds down longer than they had ever been. The sensations were short-circuiting my brain. I had my head thrown back, over stimulated. I could taste blood from where I had bitten my lip, not even realizing I had done it. My breathing was erratic and puffing out in short bursts. I could feel Jarrod's breath tickling the hair on the back of my neck. He changed his angle, hitting my prostate directly on.

"Fuck, Jarrod, please." I didn't even know what I was asking for. I just needed him to do something.

"How do you think the heads of Velatus Deus would take it if they could see their leader taking it like a bitch up the ass?" He grabbed my hair and pulled my head back. "Answer me, Eamon."

"I don't care what they think. I want your cock, and I'll kill anyone who gets in the way."

I fucking meant it. I was taking back control, and those assholes could either welcome the change or meet my personal assassin.

Jarrod ripped the cock ring off. "Your ass is too good. I have to come."

My dick was so purple and painful. Jarrod reached around and gave it two tugs, and I was jetting out cum like it had been months since I'd emptied my balls, not a day. Jarrod kept fucking me through my orgasm. His hold on my hips was tight, and every push made the clamps grip tighter. If I wasn't being held up by the cuffs and Jarrod's dick, I would be on the floor. My arms and legs were shaking from the strain.

"Fuck, Eamon. You are so fucking hot. I love fucking you."

His cock throbbed inside me, and I felt his warmth through the condom. I wish I could be filled up with his cum. I'd never trusted anyone or felt the intensity of feelings for another person as I was now with Jarrod. We spent a minute just catching our breath, then Jarrod unbuckled the cuffs and massaged my skin. He led me over to the couch, where he sat down, then pulled me so I was face down on his lap. I could smell his cum sticking to his dick and his manly sweat. I nearly leaned over and licked the sweat off his balls, but I was too sleepy to move. I felt the cool lotion of aloe vera hit my back, and Jarrod rubbed it in. It didn't hurt as much as last time.

We moved on to the sex earlier this time, both of us too aroused to prolong the scene.

I lay like that for a while, Jarrod stroking my hair. I needed to convince him that we were worth a shot. I realized I didn't even know the location of his home base.

"Where do you live when you're not working?"

"Philly, and I have an apartment in New York as well."

"Will you consider us continuing to see each other? I really want your help with Velatus Deus as well."

"I will on one condition. VD needs to change, and if I don't see that happening, I'm out. You can't be separated from VD. Your sense of responsibility will make you continue to work yourself into the ground."

"Our life will be about rules. If we establish them up front and try to always stick to them, we can make it work," I said.

"Even if it means working less hours and tightening up your security?"

"Yes, I know things have to change. I've been unhappy most of my life because I want to do things differently. I need your help to make that happen."

"Okay, let's give it a go."

I sat up and straddled his lap. "Thank you."

We kissed like lovers, softly and using our tongues, sensually sucking and licking inside each other's mouths. Our lives would be a scene of contrasts, in and out of the bedroom. I'd found the one, and it felt glorious. I'd live up to his high expectations and make this right. Otherwise, there'd be a lot of punishments in my future. I wasn't actually sure that would be a deterrent, but I'd keep that thought to myself.

"Are you ready to punish me again?" I asked.

"Yes, Eamon. Everyone loves a bad boy."

Epilogue
One

Eamon

The office didn't hold the appeal it once did. I was frequently distracted lately, and I'd found myself delegating a lot more work. I'd even employed an operations manager for my private logistics business to share the workload with. Jarrod and I shared the leadership of Velatus Deus, and we had team leaders who helped keep things running.

The reason for that distraction was just walking into my office and locking the door. Jarrod walked his sexy ass over to me, pushed my office chair back, and straddled me.

He smirked. "Are you planning on being late tonight?"

I raised my eyebrows at him. "Do we have plans?"

He started to unbutton my shirt—I'd taken my jacket off hours ago. Outside of sex or any bedroom antics, I was bossy, but as soon as my libido engaged, I was a true submissive.

I knew to stay still and not speak from this point on. Jarrod could and had punished me by getting my cock rock hard, then walking away. I had to play by the rules we'd established. Our relationship had very firm boundaries that we both enjoyed and that met our needs sexually and in our day-to-day relationship.

"Have you been a good boy today, Eamon?" Unless he said I could speak, I wouldn't answer him.

Jarrod pulled my shirt down my arms, trapping me in the material. Once it was out of the way, he started biting me down my neck and then my nipples. He licked and sucked them to take the sting away. I was covered in bite marks and bruises—Jarrod loved to mark me, and I loved to carry his marks.

Jarrod scooted back on my knees; we didn't have much room, as we were both big men. He undid my belt and pulled it until it was out of my trouser loops. My heart rate picked up. Any time he had something in his hand that could punish me, my body reacted immediately.

"You see, Eamon, I don't think you have been a good boy. It's six p.m. on a Friday, and you're still working. You've kept me waiting to go eat."

Technically that wasn't true. We usually left no later than six thirty to go eat, which was our established rule.

I wasn't going to argue, though, because he was going to give me what I wanted anyway.

Jarrod swung his leg over and jumped off me. He leaned down to my ear.

"Lie over your desk and have your fine ass up, facing me."

I shivered from the tone he used. We'd had to replace the desk with a sturdier one when we'd realized my original was not up to our adventures.

I unzipped my pants and let them slide down my hips. Most of the time I was commando for this very reason. I lay down until my cheek was flat against the desk, leaving my ass up in the air as I was instructed.

"Look at this peach of an ass." He slapped me on both cheeks with his hand, making me thrust forward.

I also had a humiliation kink, but we left that for our more intense scenes.

Without warning, Jarrod let loose with my belt and I felt the sting of the leather hitting my ass cheeks. As it slapped my ass, the euphoria of the pain surged through me.

"Ah."

The pleasure soared through my body. Jarrod wasn't hitting as hard as I could take because we were going out.

My fingers clawed at the wood of my desk as I jolted forward from the strikes. I was shaking. Pain was my kryptonite, and I went to mush when Jarrod was the one inflicting it.

"Fuck, you look hot, Eamon."

The belt was flung to the floor, and I heard the opening of the drawer where we kept the lube. Jarrod stuck two fingers in and scissored to get some stretch. I liked it to hurt, so preparation was minimal. Soon after, he was ramming me with his sizable cock.

He knew how to hit my prostate every time and milk every drop of cum from me. I wasn't allowed to come until he said. If I slipped, he would withhold any type of sexual activity for a week. The last time he did that it nearly killed me. I'd begged and pleaded, and it hadn't been pretty.

"I love watching my cock disappear inside your juicy ass."

He grabbed my hair and pulled me up. He licked up my neck and then bit me hard on the meaty part between shoulder and neck.

"Jarrod!" I yelled.

He was fucking me as hard as he could. My thighs were feeling the hits as I banged into the desk.

He reached around and grabbed my cock. Thank fuck. I hadn't been sure that I was going to make it. He gave me a few pulls and my cock exploded, cum shooting out all over the desk. He let go of my hair and I flopped forward.

Jarrod grabbed my hips and thrust twice and then came. I could feel the heat of him spilling in my ass. "Fuck yeah. Your ass is hot as hell."

He pushed on my head. "Stay down. I want to see my cum drip out of your ass." We had stopped using condoms months ago after getting tested. I pushed so it would leak out quicker. It was now dripping down my thighs.

"Jesus. I love fucking you, and that is next-level hot." He stuck his cock back in a few times. After coming, he stayed hard for a short time.

Jarrod pulled out and flopped back into my chair, then he grabbed me until I was lying on top of him. He nuzzled my neck and earlobe.

We stayed like that for a few minutes, catching our breath and enjoying being together.

"What was that bullshit about six p.m.?" I asked.

"I was hungry and horny, so sue me," he said in a grumpy voice.

I laughed. I couldn't believe I'd found the perfect guy for me. In a total twist, Jarrod now worked for Velatus Deus. He and Byrne were cleaning house and getting the place back in order. We'd changed the modus operandi to take on paid jobs that fucked up bad guys, and Jarrod had a team dedicated to human trafficking.

"I love you," I said.

He lightly bit me on the neck and sucked my skin. "Love you, too. Do you want to go again?" Jarrod said.

"I thought you were hungry."

"Only for you, babe," he whispered in my ear as he spun me around so I could ride him to our next orgasm.

Epilogue
Two

Jarrod

We'd made this trip quite a few times over the last few years. It was special in a way, since it was just for us, and it was our time to be someone else.

The seaplane banked for landing. I could see the clear blue waters of the Caribbean and, in the distance, the port of Trunk Bay welcoming us back. Eamon was at my back with his arms wrapped around me. The last five years with him had been amazing. He got me, and I knew him inside and out. We had saved lives and made Velatus Deus something to be proud of. We had even started the conversation about the possibility of kids.

As the plane docked, we saw the familiar sign of Leather Persuasion Resort. Lance waited to welcome guests, like he had for all the years we had been coming here. Eamon and I were married in our real lives, but here we were Mr. and Mr. Campbell. The only thing different from our first visit was Eamon demanded that we stay in the most luxurious of cottages. Since it came with its own BDSM room and equipment, I gave in without too much of a fuss.

Lance rushed over. "Happy anniversary, Jarrod and Eamon. I'm so glad to see you."

He hugged us, and we couldn't help but be happy to see him. This was our happy place, and we took two weeks a year around our wedding anniversary to have a break and concentrate on us.

During the year, whenever Eamon pissed me off, I thought up creative ways to punish him and played them out right here in tropical paradise. We knew the drill, and Lance quickly got us and the other guests to the resort. Being VIPs, we were treated like royalty. I rolled my eyes, while Eamon lapped it up. He thought he deserved it after all the crap he had to put up with from his two jobs. I couldn't dispute that, but I still gave him shit about being a snob.

As we entered our cottage, the Saint Andrew's cross took pride of place in the open room. I watched Eamon's face—it was one of my favorite things to watch as he submerged himself into his submissive alter ego. He started clenching his fists and licking his lips. I always made him wait to use the cross. In some ways, it was me also slipping into my dominant role that we enjoyed. Day to day in our lives and anything to do with Velatus Deus, we were equal and shared in the decision-making. In the bedroom, I was always the dominant and him the submissive. How deep we got into those roles depended on how we were feeling and how busy we were. At Leather Persuasion, it was full submersion.

I walked up behind him and wrapped my arms around his chest. "Happy fifth wedding anniversary, darling. These have been the best six years of my life, and I'm grateful for our life together and the wonderful husband that you are."

He turned in my arms to wrap me up. "Thank you for saying yes and for trusting me all those years ago when I said it would be different. You are my most important treasure."

We stayed like that for a minute, and then it was time to change to that other Jarrod—the one who was born here at this resort. That Jarrod liked to inflict pain and watch his husband break apart, and then he put the pieces back together.

I pulled back and grinned at him. He knew what was coming. "Okay, enough sappy stuff. We love each other, yeah, blah blah blah. Eamon, I have some really interesting things planned for us for the first few days, and don't be expecting to be able to sit on that hot ass for a week."

He grinned. "I'm counting on it."

This was us, and we were happy.

What do they say? Love hurts. In our case, it was literally!

Afterword

I hope you enjoyed this sidetrip from my AZ Demon's series. Please join my newsletter and socials and keep in touch.

    Go to the QR code below and sign up to my mailing list for additional scenes from the AZ Demon series and my new releases. Being part of my mailing list will also give you access to ongoing additional content and updates.

    To follow me on my socials and email click on the QR code below to my Linktree account.

About the
Author

Ash Marah is an Australian who has spent all her life reading every genre of romance novel, and thought she should have a go at writing one! Let's just say it was not that easy, but with help from some authors and friends, this dream became a reality.

As a mother of two girls, a husband, two cats and two dogs her life can get very busy, but writing is a labor of love, so she will make time to fit that in. When she is not writing or working, she is reading and enjoying all the books from her author heroes.